BEDFELLOWS

LOLA LEIGHTON

Bedfellows

Copyright © 2018 Lola Leighton

Content Editing by

Elaine York

Proofreading by

Virginia Tesi Carey

Cover Design by

Uplifting Designs

About the Book

I wasn't looking to fall for one man. Let alone two...

Sullivan and Will are as close as two friends can be. Growing up in the system forced them to rely on each other, and they've become accustomed to sharing everything—including women.

Now they're ready for more. To find love. To start a family. To see the dreams they've shared since childhood come true.

Apparently I tick off every box on their list—brains, beauty, and sass. I never hesitate to put both men in their places—which they find sexy as hell.

One problem, I'm a traditional girl, with traditional values—one man, one woman, till death do us part—kind of values.

They're willing to work to prove how very right the three of us could be, but what happens next is anyone's guess...

Friendly Warning

This book is packed with hot, passionate love that doesn't know any boundaries, so sit back, enjoy and get ready for a smutily-ever-after.

Chapter One

Sullivan

"GETTING RESTLESS," WILL GRUNTED from beside me. We were seated in the cab of my truck on our trek home after a hard day's work.

"For?" I asked, playing coy. I knew exactly what he needed. Had known for the past two months he was ready. Though to be fair, I knew him like the back of my hand. I'd been waiting for this conversation for a while, and found it amusing that he was finally bringing it up.

"Need a woman," he murmured, his gaze locked on the horizon out the front windshield.

"You need a fucking shower is what you need," I returned.

He shook his head beside me, flipping down the visor when the evening setting sun hit him. "Not right now. Not tonight. But soon."

"I know," I swallowed a sigh. "Me, too."

We'd been doing the same song and dance for the last decade, because Will and I—we shared everything—

including women.

We'd grown up together, two lost, angry kids banding together to forge a path through a fucked-up world. It made us strong, made us brave—made us the men we were today. But it made us rely on each other in a way that was … a little out of the ordinary.

In our teens, we'd explored porn together, in our twenties, we'd experienced our first threesomes, and now in our thirties, we owned a home together, sure enough in ourselves and our friendship that we know preferred monogamy—a shared relationship with the same woman.

I was confident enough in my sexuality to admit this probably meant I was bi—Will, not so much. We didn't talk about our needs, didn't share our deep, inner thoughts on the subject. In fact, these days we were mostly on auto-pilot. But the important thing was—we were each happy with what we had—a kick-ass friendship, a solid business, and the desire to fuck the same woman. It worked. We didn't question it. End of story. And life was good—this dry spell aside.

However, finding someone who suited us both was sometimes a challenge. Which is why and how we found ourselves in our current situation.

I shot him a questioning glance. "You miss Layla?"

Maneuvering my truck toward the pub where we often called in to-go orders before we left whichever house we were currently rehabbing, I waited while he weighed the question.

"No, not really," he breathed, still looking ahead.

That was a relief. When things had ended a few months ago, I'd been pleased. She wasn't the one. She was too much drama—too much work, and deep down, she didn't make either of us happy. Not really.

As we got closer to the restaurant, my stomach began to grumble. We took turns cooking, but when it was Will's night to cook, we usually had take-out. Rotating between Thai, sushi, or our favorite, burgers from McGilley's pub.

"You want to go in for a beer, or are we just going to wait in the truck?" Will asked.

"We have beer at home. That IPA you like. And I meant it when I said you need a fucking shower." I shot him a grin. We'd spent the day ripping out cabinets and demoing walls.

"That's fair." He chuckled under his breath. "I'll go in and check on the order, be back in a few."

"Sounds good." The pub had incredibly fast service and it wasn't like we were ordering anything complicated. It should only take ten minutes or so.

Will hopped out and I maneuvered my truck toward a parking spot further down. My truck was a brand new, black, platinum edition with the chrome grill I'd spoiled myself with after the sale of my last successful real estate project. After growing up with nothing, it was tough to break out of that mindset. Every dollar was hard-earned, and watching them slowly grow in my bank account was generally more satisfying than blowing it on stuff. Stuff never made you happy. Aside from my truck. My truck was my fucking baby.

Wham.

My truck spun sideways into a hard stop while my brain took a moment to understand what had just happened.

"Fuck!" I grunted out. Some red little sedan had just crashed into the bed of my truck. Slamming the gearshift into park, I hoped out to inspect the damage.

A woman stepped out of the sedan. She was trembling, and clearly knew she had messed up. I had no idea whether she was about to cry or curse.

"Shit!" she groaned.

Curse it was.

"Are you okay, Miss?" I asked, walking closer. Even as pissed off as I was at the moment, I could see she was a twelve out of ten. Curvy with long legs, a trim little waist, and honey-blonde hair that framed a heart-shaped face.

"I'm fine. I'm so sorry. It's been one of those days, you know." She wrung her hands in front of her, looking nervous, probably waiting for me to blow up and yell at her.

I bent down, looking at the rear quarter-panel on my truck and winced. It was dented, but the damage was less than what I was expecting. I let out a heavy sigh and turned to look at the woman standing beside me. Now that I was calmer I took a minute to notice how utterly gorgeous she was.

A full, plush mouth and big brown eyes that were currently wide with worry. She didn't wear much make-up, but shit, she didn't need it.

She was dressed in a pair of ripped-up jeans that might have been worth more than her car for all I knew, a white t-shirt knotted at her waist, and a pair of high-heeled boots.

"You sure you're okay?"

She nodded. "I mean, no. Not really. But I'll survive, right? I always do somehow."

At this, my brow knitted in confusion.

"That's my salon." She pointed to the far end of the shopping plaza to a modern white brick structure on the end with a bright fuchsia front door. The sign above it said Studio Ten. "A pipe burst early this morning and flooded the whole place. It started in my apartment above the salon. And then my car, it's such a piece—I wasn't looking while I fiddled with the air conditioner. Totally my fault. I'm so sorry."

I shook my head. "No big deal. Accidents happen."

The woman's eyes widened again like she couldn't quite believe I wasn't going to unload a string of curse words on her. And I might have, because dude, my truck was my fucking baby. But I sensed this stranger had been through enough today.

"Let me get my ID and insurance card." She rushed toward her car, shouting over one slender shoulder, "We can exchange information."

I nodded and waited for her to return. "I'm Sullivan. Didn't catch your name."

"It's Adrienne Edmonds," she said, offering me a small smile.

"Placed our order," Will said, wandering back to stop beside us. His eyes zeroed in on the damage to my truck. "Everything okay?" Will knew exactly how much my truck meant to me, so I was guessing his tempered response was her benefit—as not to freak out the pretty stranger.

"Will, this is Adrienne. Adrienne…Will."

Will reached one hand toward her. "Hey, there. You alright, Adrienne?"

She returned his handshake, her entire hand disappearing within his firm grasp.

"I feel like an ass, but other than that, yeah. Perfectly fine."

"Have you eaten yet?" I asked her.

Adrienne's pretty full lips parted, and she looked between Will and me. "Um, no. I was just leaving work."

I nodded. "That's what I thought. Come join us. We can get all this sorted. But I'm starved."

She was still clutching her driver's license and insurance card in her hands, and her expression changed to one of confusion.

"We could probably all use a drink right about now, too," I added.

For a second, I thought she might refuse, but instead she took a deep breath, her posture softening. "Okay. Let me park my car and I'll text my friend. She's expecting me later."

Will stayed decidedly quiet beside us, but I could feel the weight of his gaze.

What the fuck are you up to? He seemed to ask while Adrienne parked her car beside my truck.

You'll see. I wiggled my eyebrows.

Adrienne climbed from her car and started toward the restaurant.

I couldn't help but notice the way Will's gaze zeroed

in on the curve of her ass as she walked, or the slight smile that twitched on his mouth. This girl was ticking off everything on our list, and I couldn't wait to see where this could go.

Tonight just got a whole lot more interesting.

Chapter Two

Adrienne

WHAT A FREAKING DAY.

I followed my new companions, Will and Sullivan, inside the dark little pub, taking their lead toward a booth in the back. I couldn't believe I'd been so careless and crashed right into his truck like that. I'd never been in a car accident in my entire life. I was embarrassed and already stressing about how much this was going to cost me.

"Hi, there." A waitress approached us as we slid into the seats—the guys next to each other, leaving one side of the booth for me.

"We already ordered a couple of burgers, but can you change our order for here instead of to-go?" Will asked the waitress.

"'Course," the waitress replied.

I grabbed the sticky menu and looked over it quickly while the guys added a couple of beers to their order.

"The chicken tacos, please. And a large margarita," I

said.

"Coming right up." The waitress grinned at the guys again before darting away.

I had no idea why I was here sitting at dinner with them when I'd just crashed into the guy's nice, new truck. Sullivan he said his name was. I wasn't sure if that was his first or his last name, but it fit him regardless.

I pressed my palms against the table and took a deep breath. "Listen, about your truck ..." I started.

Sullivan waved a hand in my direction. "It's all good. Please don't worry about it. I over-reacted before. My buddy owns an auto-repair shop. And he owes me a couple of favors. Seriously, don't worry."

He actually didn't overreact at all. He was very calm about it, which actually made me feel worse. He could have yelled, screamed and cursed at me, but he hadn't.

I leaned back in my seat, distracted by the view in front me. Two gorgeous men. And Sullivan didn't seem mad in the least. I'd expected him to be angry at me, not trying to make me feel better.

Sullivan's right arm was adorned with ink that started at his wrist and disappeared under the edge of his t-shirt.

He was tall and somewhat lean, like a swimmer's build. His hair was a little too long on top and light brown. His eyes were friendly, and his posture relaxed. Much more relaxed than I'd expect for someone who just got in a car accident.

His friend Will was his opposite, and the more serious of the two. Darker, somehow. Brooding, almost. His dark brown hair was cropped close—like he preferred not to fuss with it, and his gray eyes tracked my every movement.

My stomach tightened into a knot.

I was grateful when our waitress reappeared, and I sucked down a large swallow of margarita. The moment the tequila and lime hit my stomach, it was as though my shoulders physically dropped as I felt myself relax into the leather booth.

"So … what happens next?" I asked, cautiously.

Sullivan smiled while Will continued to watch me with that dark, sexy stare I was already becoming a bit addicted to.

"In regard to?" Sullivan asked.

I pushed my ID and insurance card across the table toward him, but Sullivan shook his head.

"Put those back in your purse. I told you, it's all good. Let's just enjoy a beverage and a nice meal together."

"That's it?" I asked.

Sullivan shrugged, running one hand through his messy hair, making his bicep jump as he flexed. "Sometimes fate has a funny way of bringing people together."

"Fate, huh?" I asked, taking another healthy sip of my margarita. I didn't think crashing my car into his was fate's way of bringing us together, but his take on the world was refreshing.

Although, fate had not exactly been my friend lately. It seemed like all I'd had lately was bad luck. Business was great, so I couldn't complain there. I felt blessed to own my own salon at a young age, but most times I felt overwhelmed. Like I was slowly drowning. And with the pipe that burst and flooded my apartment above the salon, I'd be crashing on my friend's couch for the foreseeable future. But his attitude, combined with this margarita, was taking my rather shitty day and making it a little brighter.

"Fate," Sullivan confirmed. "Although, I do feel bad that you have to have dinner with us in our current state." He made a point of looking down at his worn t-shirt and jeans. "We came straight from work."

"What do you guys do?" I asked.

"We own a real estate investment company," Will said, finally contributing something to the conversation. He struck me as the strong, silent type. The type of man who was content to observe those around him, who only spoke when necessary, not one driven with the need to hear himself talk, but only when it added to the conversation. There was something I liked about that.

Sullivan shrugged. "We flip houses. It's a pretty good gig."

There had to be something so satisfying about working with your hands, about the transformation that made happen. I enjoyed the same thing about being a stylist. "That sounds like fun. How long have you been doing that?"

The two men looked at each other, both attempting

to calculate the amount of time that had passed since they began their business venture. "About five years now," Sullivan said.

Our food was delivered a moment later and the second the scent of grilled chicken and pico de gallo hit my nostrils, my stomach rumbled. I didn't quite realize how hungry I was. A long day of working while standing on my feet tended to do that to me. I was usually ravenous by the end of the day.

"Please, dig in," Sullivan encouraged, and it was all the invitation I needed.

I helped myself to a big bite of a chicken taco, wiping my mouth on a paper napkin. I couldn't help the moan that escaped as I chewed.

Both men immediately exchanged a look that I couldn't decipher, and my heart rate picked up.

Will asked about my work, and I filled them in on the salon while we ate.

"I know I said it before, but I really am sorry about your truck," I offered Sullivan one last time.

He smiled. "Already told you, it's all good. But …" he paused, wiping his mouth with a paper napkin. "If you want to make it up to me, you could go out with us sometime."

At this, I stopped, setting down a half-eaten taco, my eyes jumping between them. He'd said *us*, hadn't he? I couldn't have imagined it. "Both of you?" I asked. Surely there had to be some kind of misunderstanding.

Sullivan smiled at my obvious lack of understanding. "We like to stick together."

"But you guys don't look …" I stopped, sure I was about to embarrass myself.

"Don't look what?" Will asked, his tone sharp.

"Bi-sexual?" Sullivan supplied with a half-smile.

"Um … gay," I blurted.

Sullivan barked out a laugh while Will rolled his eyes so hard I thought they might get permanently lodged back there.

And truly they didn't. I knew it was stereotypical of me, but one of my best stylists at the salon was a gay man, and one whom I adored, but he was so feminine—so much different than the men seated before me. Tyler was all skin-tight jeans and an overly high voice. He had pink highlights in his hair and has been known to steal my lip-gloss. These men were rugged, rough around the edges, and also freaking huge—well over six feet tall, both of them with plenty of defined muscle.

"That's because we're not," Will answered.

"Nope. Never fucked a dude before." Sullivan shook his head.

Will bit out a laugh, then chugged down a sip from his beer.

"So why do all this? I don't get it, I mean …"

"That's a story for another time," Will said, his eyes darting to Sullivan's before coming to rest on mine again.

A moment of silence passed and I couldn't help but feel a small, silent agreement was being made as the men made eye contact.

"Go out with us," Sullivan said again, his voice soft, sweet.

I'd only been in their company for a matter of minutes, and already they had me so twisted up, I didn't know which way was up.

"I'm sorry, no." I fiddled with the straw in my

margarita, fingers trembling. I'd only known them for thirty minutes—and we'd met under less-than-ideal circumstances—but they had me more frazzled than a priest in a strip club.

"Can I ask why?" Sullivan asked.

"You aren't attracted to us?" Will asked. He'd only taken a few bites of his food, seemingly more interested in studying me and each of my reactions to them. I could honestly say I'd never met a man like him before. My ex was interested in just about anything but sitting and talking to me—scarfing down his food, playing with his phone, those damn video games he loved. And Will was … simply different.

If I wasn't so thrown off, and slightly intrigued, maybe I could have thought it through more clearly, achieved a more articulate response to their question. But the fact was, I was overwhelmed by the very idea of them and their proposition. Had I had more time to think about what they were asking, I'd be overflowing with questions like why me? What do you mean, go out with both of you? At the same time? Separately but date them both? Obviously they want to have sex but does that mean with both of them, at the same time, or with one watching, or,

… There were way too many pieces in the Will and Sullivan puzzle, it had my brain glitching.

I had to admit to myself, though, that of course, I was interested. They were both physically beautiful, each in their own way. But I was a simple girl and these types of relationships and all that it would or could entail didn't exist in my reality. Period.

I took a deep breath, sure my cheeks were now flushed. "I just … two men? No. I can't."

I might have seemed easy-going and up for anything, but deep down, I just wasn't built that way. I'd grown up in a strict, southern Baptist family in the heart of Texas. I'd left all that behind, but somewhere deep down inside of me, I was still very much a traditional girl—a one man, one woman, till death do us part—kind of girl.

Not that they were proposing marriage. *Get a grip, Adrienne.* They weren't proposing anything more than one night of fun between the sheets. But even that was too much for me. I'd never had a one-night stand in my entire life, and I wasn't about to start now. And certainly not with two men.

Were they just proposing one night? My head and my

emotions were all over the place right now.

Sullivan held up his hands. "I'm sorry, I didn't mean to overwhelm you. I just … you're beautiful. I read things wrong between us. I thought maybe you'd be interested."

"In what? Sharing your bed for the night? I'm sorry, that's not me."

Will shook his head. "We don't do the one-and-done thing."

At this, my interest picked up. "What do you mean?"

Sullivan continued. "We share everything—a home, our business, and yes, women. But we do so inside of a committed, monogamous relationship. We aren't looking for a hookup."

"Oh." I had no idea if that made me feel better or worse. But the butterflies inside my stomach took flight again.

"It's just dinner. Come out with us, and we'll talk about it." Sullivan's eyes sparked with mischief as he spoke.

Looking back and forth between them, their eye contact seemed genuine and sincere.

"I'll think about it." Since I knew I wasn't going to get anything else out of them, I focused on my plate, taking another bite of a chicken taco.

"You have to. Go out with us, I mean," Sullivan said. "The tacos here are a sad excuse for Mexican food. You need to let us take you to Felix's Taco Hut."

I raised one brow. "Taco Hut? That sounds dreamy."

"Oh, it's not. Don't get your hopes up. It's a hole in the wall, but their tacos are killer," he added.

One more glance between them—these two sexy, masculine men—and I realized they probably weren't going to let this go. I could tell they were the kind of men who pursued what they wanted with dogged determination, the type who never lost. And this tingling curiosity I felt deep inside my chest refused to fade, in fact it got stronger with every heartbeat. I swallowed hard and drew a deep breath. "What the hell. I'll go." I shrugged.

Sullivan chuckled. "Now that's the spirit. You free on Friday?"

My gaze wondered over toward Will's in an attempt to see how he felt about all of this.

He was still watching me intensely. Still making my

insides feel like Jell-O.

"Say yes, sweetheart. We don't bite," Will said finally.

"Yes. I'm free on Friday." The words felt thick in my throat. It was a few simple words, but their meaning was huge. I was saying yes to this—to a date with two men. When so many questions were dangling there, unspoken, unasked. But for once I was going to trust my gut instinct and see what this was all about, then I could decide for myself. If it was totally weird and uncomfortable, I never had to see them again.

When the bill came, Sullivan snatched it before Will could, and though I protested, they insisted on paying. I didn't put up much of a fight. The repair bills at my shop were going to ensure I lived on a pretty tight budget for a while. After signing the credit card tab and adding a generous tip, Sullivan handed the check back to the waitress.

After exchanging phone numbers, we all rose and walked to the exit together.

"We'll pick you up at seven," Sullivan said.

Determined to maintain some level of independence in case things went south, I shook my head. "I'll meet you there."

"Until then," Will added, treating me to the first hint of a smile.

And just like that, I had a hot date with not one, but two men.

What in the bananas was happening to my life?

Chapter Three

Will

I LOOKED AT THE TWO DRESS SHIRTS I'd laid on my bed and scrubbed a hand over my hair.

God, why had I let Sullivan talk me into this? A glance at the clock told me we had twenty minutes before our date, and I needed to finish getting ready.

Adrienne was beautiful, yes, but from the first moment he'd laid eyes on her, he knew it would never work. Sullivan was too smitten, for one. And she didn't seem particularly interested in a ménage relationship. Which was kind of the entire fucking point.

She also looked somewhat fragile, delicate somehow—like she'd never be able to handle both of us at once. That fact didn't sit right with me.

Taking the shirts from my bed, I hung them both back inside the closet, and grabbed a t-shirt instead. Best to keep this casual. It probably wasn't going to go anywhere. We'd enjoy a nice meal, maybe some good conversation, and then send the pretty little Adrienne on her way. And that would be the end of it. Sullivan would just have to get over his little infatuation.

I met Sullivan in the living room where he sat, nursing a beer with the sports highlights playing low in the background.

He was dressed in a light blue polo and dark jeans. I felt his gaze roam over my attire, and I waited for him to chastise my choice of outfit.

But he didn't.

He just took another swig of his beer and looked back at the TV. "Raiders lost again. Does that mean you owe José another twenty?"

I grunted an affirmative. It was a stupid bet I'd made with one of our contractors, but it was all in good-natured fun, and the constant banter helped our workday go by that much faster.

"You about ready?" Sullivan asked, draining the last of his beer and rising to his feet.

"Yeah." I slid my feet into a pair of Vans and met his gaze. "You sure about this? She didn't seem particularly into the idea of us."

Sullivan chuckled. "She was. She just didn't know how to handle the fact that she was."

"If you say so." I grabbed my keys from the entryway table. "I'll drive."

"Keep an open mind, Will," Sullivan said, his deep voice going uncharacteristically soft. "I think she could end up being the one."

The one? He was even more smitten than I thought. That wasn't a good sign.

"We'll see." My guess was that Adrienne would think it over, feel flattered, but in the end, want nothing to do with us. The nice, normal girls were generally that way. Sure, sometimes they liked to take a walk on the wild wide—but even that was always short-lived. It was why Sullivan and I were still single, at thirty-two and thirty-four, respectively.

We arrived at the restaurant which was already getting busy with the dinner crowd. Free chips and fresh salsa combined with the best Mexican food in town meant this place could get pretty crowded on a Friday night.

After Sullivan gave his name to the hostess, we stood just inside the entryway. Him with his hands in his pockets, me fiddling with my phone. I had a brief flash of worry—what if she didn't show? Sullivan would be let down, that was for sure. I realized that I would be, too.

And then she was here—pushing through the glass door, her eyes wide as she searched through the crowd for us. Her gaze landed on Sully first, and a genuine smile twitched at her lips.

If it was even possible, she looked even more stunning than the last time.

A black pencil skirt that hugged her hips, a silky peach-colored top that draped over her tits in a way I found to be extremely distracting, and a pair of high-heeled gold sandals on her feet. Feet I'd like to see propped up on Sullivan's shoulders later.

Jesus, Will. I needed to get a hold of myself, and fast. What was it about this woman that was already pushing all my buttons, making me go from hot to cold and back again?

"You came," Sullivan said, greeting her warmly with a hug.

"I did." She smiled, her face transforming as she did. "Almost talked myself out of it at the last minute," she admitted, looking down to adjust her purse strap.

God, she was cute. All pink cheeks and fluttering eyelashes. I liked that she was nervous, and I wasn't even sure why.

"Glad you didn't." Sullivan took a step back. Social decency dictated that it was now my turn to greet her, but I wasn't a hugger, wasn't nearly as affectionate or open or giving as he was. It took me longer to warm up. It was one of the things Adrienne would learn if she stuck around for any length of time. But I wouldn't make any apologies about that. It was just how I was wired. I shifted a step closer, seemingly drawn to her in a way I couldn't quite explain.

"You look beautiful," I said, surprising myself with the sudden need for honesty between us. Maybe I was inspired by her own admission that she'd almost chickened out. But either way, the compliment earned me a smile from Sullivan, and a warm blush that spread faintly along the delicate column of Adrienne's neck.

The hostess led us to a cheery table on the patio with mosaic tiles in red, orange, and blue. Little strings of white fairy lights flickered on, giving everything a romantic vibe.

Suddenly I was no longer questioning Sullivan's choice in restaurant.

We sat down, each of us choosing an outside chair so that Adrienne had no choice but to seat herself between us. We flipped open our menus, browsing the dinner options in silence for a moment.

"So, what's good here?" Adrienne asked, directing her question to Sullivan, having already learned he was the chattier of the two of us.

"Everything," he answered. "The peach margaritas are amazing. Did you drive, or…?"

Adrienne shook her head. "My car's in the shop from the accident the other night. I had a friend drop me off. I figure I'll call for a ride later."

I shook my head, the movement capturing her attention. And damn, what a feeling to be under her gaze—hot, and confusing, and certain all at once. "I'll drop you off after. Order whatever you'd like."

Sullivan nodded. "Then you should definitely try the peach margaritas."

"So just cosmetic damage then? Everything else okay with your car?" I asked as we all folded our menus on the table.

Adrienne nodded. "It will be. They're just replacing the front bumper."

"And what about your salon, and the water damage you mentioned?" Sullivan asked.

Adrienne looked back and forth between us, seemingly unsure about how she felt being caught in this game of ping-pong.

Make that two of us.

"The contractor said it's going to be a few weeks before I can get back into my apartment. But I refuse to close the salon—or really, I just can't afford to. I've worked so hard to get here and build up my clientele, I don't like letting people down. So, we're working around the mess."

"But I don't understand, where are you sleeping then?" Sullivan asked.

Leave it to him to ask a question so personal.

Adrienne just smiled at his concern. "I'm crashing on my friend Dani's couch. It's like being in school all over again. One big slumber party." She let out a nervous chuckle.

Sullivan raised one shoulder. "That should be fun, though—a chance for girl talk and all that stuff."

At this, Adrienne shook her head. "Yeah, not so much. She and her boyfriend just recently had a baby, so it's a little chaotic there. Midnight feedings and all the exhaustion and stress of learning to care for a newborn. I mostly just feel like I'm in their way." She looked down at her hands. "I'm sorry, I don't know why I told you all that."

Sullivan reached for her hand. "It's fine. Please let me know if there's anything we can do to help. I'm happy to swing by the salon and take a look."

Adrienne nodded, and offered him another one of those heart-stopping smiles.

When the waitress swung back by, we ordered a platter of tacos and a pitcher of margaritas for Sullivan and Adrienne to share.

"What about you?" she asked.

I shrugged. "Ice water is fine."

"He's not much of a drinker," Sullivan supplied,

answering for me.

Especially not when I'm driving. But in general too, I didn't like the feeling of being tipsy. Never had. I much preferred to be in control.

Our drinks were delivered, and I watched as Adrienne brought the margarita glass to her lips, tasting the icy-liquid with a soft sigh.

"Oh, that's just sinful." She chuckled and took another sip.

Her skin was golden with the setting sun caressing her cheeks and it looked so fucking soft it almost hurt to think about what it'd feel like beneath my fingertips. Sullivan was watching her, too, and I wondered if he was thinking the same thing. I took a large gulp of ice water to cool down.

Our food was delivered quickly and we each dug in. It was nice to see a woman eat with such gusto. Nothing annoyed me more than a woman who ordered rabbit food and then picked at it while complaining about calories. I was glad to see Adrienne wasn't like that.

"Are you going to eat that?" She gestured with her fork to a side dish containing guacamole that sat untouched beside me.

"No, please." I set the little dish next to her plate, and she heaped a pile onto her taco, taking a big bite and letting out another of those soft sighs.

Sullivan shot me a grin.

The asshat. So, maybe he was right—she was perfect. Beautiful, sexy, intelligent, hard-working, the list went on. But that didn't mean she'd be interested in our lifestyle—which would obviously be a huge deal-breaker.

While we ate, Adrienne asked small-talk questions, and for the most part, Sullivan answered. About how we met—at an orphanage. How long we'd been living this lifestyle—for as long as we could remember. And then finally—how does it work.

I swallowed the final bite of my food and waited, heart picking up. Sullivan stayed quiet, no doubt wanting me to field this particular question.

Adrienne's gaze drifted from Sullivan's over to mine with a flicker of interest hidden in their blue depths.

"You interested, sweetheart?"

Chapter Four

Will

THE TEMPERATURE IN THE RESTAURANT seemed to ratchet up several degrees as Adrienne's appraising eyes danced between mine and Sullivan's. My question hung in the air around us, unanswered for several heartbeats.

Was she interested?

That was the million-dollar question.

Finally, a determined look crossed her features. "I'm not going to lie. I've thought about it. Probably more than I care to admit, even to myself." She swallowed, that slender throat working like she was more nervous than she was letting on.

My own heart picked up the pace as I waited to see what she'd say next.

"And?" Sullivan asked, elbows on the table, like he couldn't help but get closer.

Adrienne waited to speak again while the waitress cleared our dishes. "The two of you together is …"

"Impressive?" Sullivan supplied, smiling crookedly.

The bastard was always smiling, like this was some big joke. Didn't feel that way to me. It felt huge— monumental. Either she'd accept us and our lifestyle, or she wouldn't, and we'd be forced to move on yet again.

"Overwhelming," she finally answered. Adrienne cleared her throat, then fiddled with the napkin in her lap. She had more to say on the subject, and like dutiful subjects deferring to our queen, we waited. "But I also thought that it might be fun," she added softly, mouth twitching with the beginnings of a smile.

"If it's one night of fun you're looking for, like I mentioned before, we're not interested," I said, voice coming out more ragged than I intended.

Taking a breath, I fought to compose myself. It didn't matter how stunningly gorgeous she was, didn't matter that that one night of pleasure would be damn enjoyable—for all three of us—it didn't change anything. Wouldn't replace the deep ache in my chest for a partner. A life-long partner. The chance at a real future. A family.

"I know Sullivan only hinted at how we grew up, but I can promise you, it was a lot worse than anything you might be imagining. We grew up relying only on each other, it shaped us. I know it's hard to understand, and I promise we'll tell you anything you want to know. But the most basic way to explain it is that it left us with certain wants. Certain needs."

Sullivan placed his hand on her lower back as he leaned in closer. "He's right. It's not a hookup we're looking for. It's a relationship."

Finally, he'd come to his senses. It felt good to hear him back me up.

Adrienne nodded, her eyes dawning with understanding. "I get that. I'm the same way. I've never had a one-night fling in my entire life. I'm more of a serial monogamist, too. I just … I'm not sure how it would all work."

At this, Sullivan chuckled. "It's actually quite simple. Two loving, devoted boyfriends. Two men worshipping you. Bringing you pleasure. Monogamy's not the right word. But exclusivity. Just between us three."

Her cheeks colored, and her pulse picked up in her throat. Clear signals that she very much liked the idea. "Yes, but there are things to consider, like my ultra-religious parents, what my friends might say, and the logistics of it all ..."

"The logistics..." Sullivan was back to grinning at her. I could tell he'd be all-too-happy to explain the *logistics* to her in vivid detail—or better yet, offer a hands-on demonstration.

I held up one hand. "We're getting ahead of ourselves." We were talking about this like it was a forgone conclusion, and really, we hardly knew each other, hardly knew if we were compatible at all.

Sullivan nodded. "Will's right. Let's just enjoy each other's company for now and see where this goes." His tone was casual—much too casual.

"Or doesn't go," I added for good measure. "No hard feelings either way."

She nodded once and took another contemplative sip of her drink.

A moment later, Adrienne rose to her feet, excusing herself to use the ladies' room while Sullivan and I shared a glance.

"Well?" I asked once she'd disappeared around the corner. "How do you think it's going?"

The smirk that lifted one side of his mouth made me roll my eyes.

He was so goddamn obvious. I knew he wanted her. And shit, so did I, but I wasn't about to push her into something she wasn't one-hundred percent on board with. I certainly wouldn't want her to have any regrets, and I didn't want Sullivan getting in over his head and winding up heartbroken. That wouldn't be good for anyone. Least of all me.

"I like her, man. Like, *really* like her. You?"

I swallowed. "Same. But I don't know …"

He smiled and poured the last of the slushy margarita mix into each of their glasses. "Just keep an open mind."

"You, too," I encouraged. "This might not work out."

He shrugged me off. Always the damn optimist.

Dating had always been a little bit tricky for us. We'd tried a variety of tactics over the years—from just one of us pursuing a woman, and then introducing her to our desires later—which ended with varying degrees of success. To being straight up and forthright from the beginning, like with Adrienne—which is what we preferred now that we were older. Two people clicking and falling in love was an anomaly—three people? A near impossibility.

"Give it a chance," Sullivan said under his breath as we watched Adrienne approach again, her lipstick freshly reapplied.

They finished their cocktails while Sullivan told stories of some of our house-flip disasters over the years. She was beautiful when she laughed. So beautiful, that it hit me straight in the groin.

Patience, I reminded myself.

Later when the dinner crowd had cleared out, and I'd long ago paid our bill, a moment of silence settled amongst us. It was a comfortable silence. An easy silence.

Adrienne smiled at me. "Thank you for dinner."

I reached over and took her hand. "Thank you for coming."

Sullivan leaned in closer. "And for keeping an open mind."

Adrienne nodded.

"Are you ready to get out of here?" I asked.

They both rose to their feet so quickly, I could have laughed at their eagerness, if it weren't for the sudden way my jeans had gone too tight in the front. The quiet chemistry that had been building between us all night was about to come to a head. But I didn't know if it'd send Adrienne running. And the thought of Sullivan chasing after her—and leaving me behind—was fucking terrifying.

Swallowing my fears, which I told myself had no basis in reality, I helped Adrienne into the passenger seat of my SUV, while Sullivan climbed into the backseat.

"Where can I take you?" I asked.

"Oh, right." Adrienne chuckled. I knew the feeling. She'd been so caught up in *this*—in us, that she'd spaced out for a moment on the need to provide me with directions, or at least an address.

After plugging in her friend's address to my navigation system, we settled once again into one of those comfortable silences.

When I pulled to a stop a few minutes later in front of a small, one-story home, Adrienne unbuckled her seat belt, and surprised me by leaning over the console to press a kiss to my cheek.

"I had a nice time," she murmured. She smelled like tequila and peaches, and holy fuck, I wanted to taste her, to suck on her tongue until she gasped into my mouth.

Instead, I nodded, touching her cheek with my thumb. "I did, too."

After flashing me a sweet smile, she turned in her seat, leaning back to get closer to Sullivan. *Lucky bastard.* From the corner of my eye, I saw him place his hand on her jaw and draw her closer.

The half-erection that had been threatening all night turned into a full hard-on as I watched him guide her mouth to his.

Their kiss was brief, just as brief as her lips on my cheek had been, and then she was placing her purse strap on her shoulder.

Her cheeks were rosy now, her eyes stormy. "You two make a tempting offer. I'll give you that."

Sullivan and I exchanged a look. I still had no idea which way she was going to go.

"So, try it. What's the worst that could happen?" Sullivan asked.

I knew very well what's the worst that could happen—a couple of broken hearts and too much whiskey, but I kept my mouth shut while Adrienne thought it over. It was her decision to make and I wouldn't push her.

"If we do this ... if I agree to date both of you, I need to set some ground rules. I feel like I should go out with each of you separately at first. Just to make sure we each have chemistry. That everything is…"

"Yes," Sullivan said.

I felt like slugging him. That had never been part of our arrangement before. Instead, I found myself nodding along. *What the fuck?* "Whatever makes you feel more comfortable."

"Okay. Well, goodnight," she murmured, pressing one last kiss to each of our cheeks before climbing out of the SUV. Sullivan climbed out behind her and walked her to the front door. Seeing them huddled together did something to me, and I watched as she unlocked the door, and then gave a little wave toward me.

I didn't realize how much I missed her scent— something subtle and slightly fruity until she'd taken it with her.

Once she was safety inside, Sullivan returned to the car, climbing into the front seat beside me.

"You think she'll be okay crashing there?" I asked as we both took one last look at the house.

Sullivan didn't respond right away, either thinking it over, or just otherwise distracted by the kiss she'd given each of us. "I'm sure she's fine. She looks like she can handle more than she lets on."

I murmured my agreement and pulled onto the road.

"Dibs on the first date," Sullivan said as I turned out of the neighborhood.

I took a deep breath, releasing it slowly. Already we were breaking our fucking rules. What was next?

Chapter Five

Sullivan

"Technically this is our third date, so does that mean I'm getting lucky tonight?" I asked.

Adrienne rolled her eyes. "Aren't you just a peach?"

I shrugged. "Life's too short. I say what I'm feeling, and I never bullshit."

"That's actually refreshing."

We'd spent the last half hour touring her little salon—it was after hours—and I told her I'd assess the damage and help out any way I could. But honestly, she'd hired a great crew and the repair work seemed to be coming along nicely. It would just take a while—completely rewiring the building so it was up to code, waiting for it to be inspected, then hanging drywall, and installing new flooring—it needed to be gutted from top to bottom. She insisted that her little apartment above would be the last thing to be fixed up and that she was fine crashing on her friend's couch, but I had my doubts that that was true.

After the tour, Adrienne turned to face me, leveling me with those big blue eyes. "And what is it that you're feeling?"

I placed my hands on her slender hips, hauling her closer. Not close enough to feel what she was doing to me, but close enough. "You. Very much."

She swallowed and looked down at her peep-toe pumps. "But you hardly know me. I'm just some chick who played bumper-cars with your truck and lost."

I shrugged. "But what I know, I like."

"What do you like?"

"You're beautiful. Independent, driven. And best of all, open-minded."

This earned me a laugh. "Yes, very, apparently."

"You ready to get out of here and head to dinner?" I asked.

Adrienne nodded, and flipped off the lights at the front of the shop before locking up.

I was impressed with the place. Despite its current state—I could see she ran an upscale salon and spa. It was all leather and wood and iron chandeliers. It was impressive that she'd been able to open her own business at such a young age, and that was just another thing to appreciate about her.

I ushered us to my now fixed-up truck and helped her climb inside. I couldn't help the glimpse I stole of her curves. Her ass was just begging for my hands, but for now at least, I minded my manners.

We had a casual dinner at the park—choosing a random food truck on both the menu and also what looked least likely to serve up a side of food poisoning.

Adrienne laughed as we stood in line to order our food. Perusing the menu, we decided to order several items and share. Asian dumplings and spring rolls and a side of stir-fried noodles, it all smelled terrific, and I loved that she had a hearty appetite. Will and I both liked to eat, and so a dainty woman who only picked at things would never work.

After sitting down at a nearby picnic table, I tapped my water bottle against hers. "Cheers."

"To?" she asked, smiling sweetly at me.

"To finding the one."

"Or the *two*." She winked.

"Exactly." I laughed as I dug into my food.

Adrienne helped herself to a bite of noodles, grinning as she chewed.

The rest of the date went like this—just easy, and comfortable. We shared small talk and some laughter, all of it coming so naturally. After we finished our food, we strolled the park hand in hand and bought some seed to scatter for the ducks in the pond. Adrienne laughed and picked out names for the baby ducklings. And God, it was crazy, but I could already see her being an amazing mother. I could picture her, full with our baby—either mine or Will's—it wouldn't matter. Her belly round and full, her cheeks glowing, she would be beautiful.

Growing up without much of anything—we wanted it all. A wife, kids, big family Christmases, all the cozy holidays and family traditions we never got to experience. It was crazy because I hardly knew her, but I just had this unmistakable gut feeling that maybe Adrienne would be the one to make those dreams a reality.

Will would say I was getting ahead of myself, but I couldn't shake this feeling. It made me want to be even more careful with her than usual, to cherish her and treasure each moment. It was like I would look back on this time fifty years from now, and I wanted to memorize each little thing.

As the sun was setting I led us back to my truck and once again helped her inside. I started it up, the low hum of the radio in the background.

"The night's still young. You want to come see our place before I drop you off?"

Adrienne smiled and nodded, shyly. "Sure. Why not."

I had no idea what might happen back at our place, but that didn't stop my knuckles from turning white as I gripped the steering wheel the entire ride back home.

I maneuvered my truck into the driveway and stopped.

"Wow. This is great." Adrienne's wide brown eyes seemed to take in every detail. From our neat, two-story brick home, to the big grassy yard, to the little flower boxes in front that Will kept meticulously weeded, her eyes were soaking it all in.

I wasn't surprised to find Will's car gone, as he'd told me he'd be out tonight.

Once inside, we slipped off our shoes and I poured Adrienne a glass of wine. Carrying her wine from room to room, she followed me as I gave her a tour.

"We bought it three years ago. Got it for a steal. It was in horrible shape."

"So, you guys restored it?"

I nodded. "With our own two hands. Top to bottom."

Her gaze cast around the open concept living and dining rooms, and I knew she was appreciating our attention to detail. The dark wood floors and soft gray walls, the built-ins surrounding the natural stone fireplace. Our home was our castle, and the one place we splurged. Neither of us was much into clothes or gadgets. But a nice faucet, walk-in closets, a couple of pieces of art on the walls, we happily invested here in our home.

"It's beautiful," she said as I showed her the first-floor master—which belonged to Will. The second bedroom on this floor had been converted into a home gym, and we merely peeked inside before continuing the tour.

"Up here is where I spend most of my time," I said,

guiding her up the stairs with my hand resting on the small of her back. The pair of jeans she wore tonight hugged her ass, and I had to force myself to look away before I went rock hard.

The second floor held two more bedrooms—mine, plus a guest room, and an open loft area with a large TV and two comfy couches.

Adrienne surveyed our surroundings, sipping her wine. "It's beautiful. It fits you perfectly."

"You think so?"

She nodded as I led us to one of the sofas. Adrienne sat beside me, clutching the stem of her wineglass in her hands.

She looked so sweet, so innocent, and nervous and lovely.

Jesus, I wanted her.

"So … I know you wanted to do this—test drive us each separately to be sure we had chemistry …"

"Test drive?" She broke into nervous laughter.

"Sorry. Wrong choice of words." I took her wineglass from her hands and placed it on the coffee table. "Tell me what you're thinking. I want you to be completely honest with me."

"Tonight has been great, Sullivan. It's just, when I think about adding Will into the equation, I get …"

"Scared?"

She shook her head. "Butterflies."

"Butterflies are good, right?"

"I think so." Her voice was barely above a whisper. I leaned in closer, captivated by her. Everything about her drew me in—from the swell of her full lips, to her uncertainty about this, and especially her willingness to try.

"He's not here now. Put the butterflies away."

"Okay." She smiled.

I leaned in closer. "I've wanted to kiss you all night."

She wet her lower lip with the tip of her tongue and it was all the answer I needed. She wanted this, too. Wanted me.

My heart pumped faster with that secret knowledge.

Tilting her chin so that her lips met mine, I took her

mouth. Gently at first, and then with a growing sense of hunger as her warm, wet tongue came out to meet mine.

She tasted incredible. Slightly sweet from the wine, and feminine and simply perfect.

"Sull..." she moaned as my lips broke from hers.

"Yes?"

"I..." she started, but then stopped herself, leaning in toward me again and pressing her full mouth to mine. I happily obliged, kissing her again. This wasn't just chemistry, this was explosive.

I was lost to her. Tongues and lips and soft, happy moans of pleasure. Finally, I pulled back again. "Can I touch you?"

A shy smile. A slight nod of her head.

Pressing my lips to her throat, I cupped her breasts in my hands, loving the soft weight of them in my palms. They were large enough to fill my hands, but not too-large, and just right for her small frame.

She moaned again as I massaged her perfect tits.

"Can we take this off?" I asked, beginning to pull at the little buttons on her shirt.

She nodded and helped me, pulling the top off over her head. The sight of her sitting on my couch wearing nothing but those jeans and a lacy lavender bra was enough to let me die a happy man.

The splotches of pink across her chest, the dip in her belly, the little knot of her belly button. God, I wanted to taste every inch of her. Wanted to plant wet kisses over her skin, working my way from her head to her toes. Instead, forcing myself to go slow, I continued kissing her—deep licks and sucks of my tongue against hers for what felt like an eternity—until she was grinding and whimpering, her body begging for more.

I undid the button on the front of her jeans, but before I went any further, I needed to see her eyes. Needed to know this was okay. Pulling back, I gazed at her. Adrienne offered me a faint nod, and it was all the assurance I needed. I worked my hand into the front of her pants, down into her panties where I felt her warm and wet and silken.

I couldn't believe she was already so wet for me, it only made my cock harder.

I rubbed the firm, swollen bud of her clit, enjoying

the soft pants and moans she made as we kissed.

"You like that?" I asked, my mouth resting against hers.

"So much," she moaned, moving her hips as my fingers continued working against her wet flesh.

I didn't dare take her pants off completely. The desire to fuck her—to thrust into her hot, wet center over and over again until I had emptied myself inside her was nearly overpowering. Will would never forgive me, and I wouldn't do that to him. Tonight wasn't about taking what I wanted, it was about giving all the pleasure I could to this sweet, beautiful woman. Besides Will and I had made an agreement—and these were the rules of engagement. Touching her, making her feel good—those were all things on tonight's menu. Fucking her without Will here was definitely not.

I pressed one thick finger inside her and Adrienne squirmed against my hand. I began fucking her with my finger, rubbing the heel of my palm against her clit and her cries of pleasure grew louder.

"Jesus, you're tight," I whispered against her lips. "You would feel so good riding my cock."

Her eyes fell closed, and she made a soft whimpering sound that hit me straight in the chest.

"You like the idea of that, baby? Riding me while Will fucks your mouth?"

She came quickly, much faster than I expected—in little trembling gasps, her fingernails digging in to my shoulders. I kissed her the entire time, her tongue reaching out to explore mine as little shudders pulsed through her petite frame.

And when her orgasm finally subsided, I pulled my fingers from her panties and brought them to my mouth, tasting her wetness.

"Fuck, you taste so good." I groaned.

"That was…" Her voice was hardly more than a shaky whisper, and she watched me with wide, hazy eyes.

"I like making you feel good," I murmured, placing one more soft kiss against her mouth. "But unless you want me to embarrass myself by coming in my jeans, we need to stop now."

The faint lush of her cheeks, the nod of her head. "Don't you want me to…"

I shook my head. "There'll be time for that. I don't want to hog you all to myself. Go on your date with Will. Then we'll talk about going further."

She nodded and straightened her clothes.

We shared one last sweet kiss, and later when I drove her back to her friend Dani's, I was happy to see there was no awkwardness between us.

When I stopped on the street in front of the house, Adrienne met my eyes.

"I had a great time tonight," I said, truly meaning it.

"I did, too." She met my eyes, a mischievous glint in them.

I laughed, and pulled her in for another kiss.

Adrienne glanced toward the house with trepidation, and then back at me.

"Are you sure you're okay staying here?" I asked, picking up on her hesitancy to go inside.

She shrugged. "It's a little cramped. Dani and her boyfriend are still adjusting to having a baby. But I need the insurance check to go toward the repairs at my salon, not toward crashing in a hotel for the next two or three weeks. I put every dime of my savings into opening the salon."

I placed my hand on her knee, giving it a reassuring squeeze. "I think it's amazing that you opened your own business. Just let us know if there's anything we can do to help."

My wheels were already turning, and though I knew it would probably freak Will out, and he'd probably try to convince me that I was going way too fast, I wanted to tell Adrienne she could stay with us while her apartment was being renovated.

Chapter Six

Adrienne

STEPPING THROUGH the front door, I was met by the distinct smell of baby spit-up. "Hey, girl," I greeted Dani who was sitting on the couch with a sleeping baby in her lap.

She looked down at the baby and put a finger to her lips.

"Sorry," I whispered. "I didn't think you'd still be up."

She nodded. "Bella just fell back asleep."

I left my shoes by the door, and joined her on the couch, leaning over to sneak a peek of the sweet newborn in her arms.

"Are you doing okay?" she asked. Dani had always been extremely perceptive, and though these past few weeks since giving birth to her daughter had taken their toll, I wasn't all that surprised that she was more concerned with what was going on with *me* than her own topsy-turvy life.

I sucked in a deep inhale and let it out slowly. "I don't even know where to start."

"You went on a date tonight, right? Was it bad, or …?"

I shook my head, folding my legs underneath me on the couch. "It was good. Like, different … good. But I have something to tell you, and I'm not sure how you'll react. Honestly though, I could really use some advice."

Dani rose from the couch and carefully placed the baby inside her bassinet in the master bedroom, taking care not to wake her. Then she re-joined me on the couch. "Tell me what's going on."

"Well, things have just gotten complicated. Tonight I went out with Sullivan."

Her brows pinched together. "What happened to Will? I thought you said you guys had a good time."

I nodded. "We did. Will and Sullivan are friends, actually." I'd only mentioned bits and pieces of my dates with them so far, making it sound like they were separate events, instead of us having dinner all together.

Her lips pressed into a firm line. "Dating two friends

... that seems like a recipe for disaster. No offense."

My stomach tingled with nerves. I wasn't explaining this well. I knew Dani wouldn't judge me, but still, this wasn't the easiest thing to admit. "They live together, they share a business, and they ... um, share women."

Dani's brown eyes widened, her eyebrows darting up on her forehead. "Okay, what? I know I'm running on like four minutes of sleep in the past two days, but I'm confused."

"Yeah." I folded my hands in my lap, unable to hide the quirked-up half-smile on my mouth. "Told you. Complicated."

She blew out a slow breath and leaned back against the couch. "I'm going to need some more details here. You can't just drop a bomb like that on me."

"I know. It's crazy. I thought so, too, at first. But now that I've actually been out with them, I like them. They're so different, but each is intriguing in his own way. Sullivan is sweet, and thoughtful and sexy. He also has amazing hair." I let out a nervous chuckle.

Dani rolled her eyes. "Leave it to you to fall for a guy over his perfect hair."

I did have a thing for good hair, but I wasn't that naïve. I didn't care so much about the outside package, it was what was inside that counted.

"And Will is … well, there are no words for Will's rugged sex appeal. He's muscular as hell, and a little less heart-on-the-sleeve, a little more broody and lot more contemplative."

"So, a growly alpha. That's hard to resist. And his hair?" Dani teased.

This time I was the one rolling my eyes. "It's super short. But he does have a sexy five-o'clock shadow."

"So, are you really going to pursue this? I'm not sure what you want me to say."

She was right. It was insane. Wasn't it? Not to mention totally out of character for me. At first, I'd had a hard time wrapping my head around their entire arrangement. I couldn't figure out if they were gay or bisexual, or what the situation was.

"I want the truth. I want your advice. Half of me wants to see where this could lead, and the other half of me is scared as hell."

Dani nodded, meeting my gaze with her insightful brown eyes. "To be totally honest, I get that. But I'm worried it could lead to heartbreak."

I pressed my lips together, knowing she wasn't nearly done, and that I had no rebuttal for that argument anyway, because deep down, I feared the exact same thing.

After drawing a deep breath, Dani continued, "I worry about what happens when you spend more time or give extra attention to one man, and the other gets jealous."

I shook my head. "They said they don't have jealousy issues."

Dani smirked. "And you believed them? Despite what they might have promised you, men are territorial creatures. It's part of their biology, their evolutionary makeup. Things are bound to turn ugly if someone feels slighted."

I chewed on my lip, unsure of how to respond. Part of me knew Dani was right, it would be a totally natural reaction to feel left out if I wasn't careful to divide my attention equally between them.

Dani leaned closer, meeting my eyes again. "Say this does work—no one's jealous, and you're all having fun…but what happens if you fall in love with one of them, and not the other?"

My stomach twisted. That thought had never occurred to me. They were a package deal, and if I chose one of them, and not the other, it could end their friendship. I'd either have to walk away, and suffer the consequences of heartbreak, or deal with the knowledge that I was responsible for driving a twenty-year friendship into the ground. Both outcomes were bleak. My stomach tightened into an intricate knot.

"I—I'm not sure," I admitted, softly.

"I just worry about you, Adrienne."

I nodded. "It'll be okay. You better go get some sleep. You need it."

Dani cleared her throat and rose from the couch. I sensed there was more she wanted to say, but for now, she kept it to herself. Then she placed her hand on my shoulder and met my eyes. "You'll figure it out. You always do."

I nodded. "Goodnight. Thanks for the advice." I

licked my lips and watched her wander back toward her bedroom.

The house was totally silent as I grabbed a sheet and blankets and started turning the couch into my bed. By the time I had changed my clothes and brushed my teeth, my brain was full-on spinning with the things Dani had said. Here in the darkness, practically homeless, her warnings felt all the more dire. All that stuff about men being territorial actually made sense.

But I had such a great time going out to dinner with them both, and then on my solo date with Sullivan. Just like I'd told Dani, he seemed like the more open and playful of the two. A smile graced my lips as I settled in, laying my head against the pillow.

Tomorrow was my first one-on-one date with Will. It was crazy how excited and nervous I felt about being alone with him next. I couldn't help but wonder how it would all work out with two men. Was I crazy like Dani said?

Deciding the best thing I could do was to try and get some sleep, I closed my eyes and said a silent prayer that maybe this wouldn't all be as complicated as it seemed. I had a full day of clients tomorrow, plus I had to meet with the insurance adjustor. I had to "adult" tomorrow and mentally spinning over what-ifs wasn't productive in the least.

I needed to keep my head on straight and not get too caught up in these men when I didn't even know if it would work out anyway. But it was easier said than done.

Chapter Seven

Will

"KEEP YOUR HIPS SQUARE. Don't lock your elbows," I instructed, watching her form. But damn, Adrienne didn't need it.

She stepped right up, raised the handgun, her form perfect, and fired—without so much as flinching.

What the hell? That was unexpected.

Stepping closer when she lowered the gun, we gazed down together to the end of the shooting range where the target was hanging.

"Wow. You're a perfect shot. That can't be beginner's luck."

She laughed. "No, sorry. I didn't want to spoil your lesson, but my dad's ex-military. He thought it was important I knew how to shoot in case I ever needed to defend myself."

I opened my mouth to say something—what, I didn't know—because the sight of her still holding that smoking piece of metal, her shapely ass and legs filling out those jeans perfectly? She was hitting all my targets. Literally. The blood rushing to my groin had nothing to do with the adrenaline of firing a handgun and everything to do with the woman standing beside me.

"What?" She grinned. "I'm from Texas."

"Then, please. Have at it." I gestured for her to continue, and Adrienne did, aiming and firing again and again, in an impressive display until she had emptied her clip.

Holy shit.

This woman continued to surprise me. She was both comfortable around guns, and an amazing shot. If I thought I was going to take her on a date that pushed her outside her comfort zone, I was going to have to up my game. I stared at her in amazement. She was completely comfortable, and watching me with a small, mischievous smile.

"What?" she asked, smirking.

I shook my head, returning her smile. "Nothing."

There was nothing quite like the feel of steel, the smell of gunpowder, or the fire power in the palm of your hand to get the blood pumping, but after a few more rounds, we were done. We turned in our handguns and went to retrieve our targets.

"Dinner?" I asked.

She offered me one of those sweet smiles again—the kind that completely disarmed me, tore down all my walls, and scared the fuck out of me.

"Absolutely. What are you in the mood for?"

"Anything but Mexican," I said, leading her out into the parking lot where my SUV was parked.

"Why? Don't tell me you don't like Mexican food," Adrienne teased, still grinning at me.

"Of course, I do. It's just that we fed you tacos during our first two dates. I'm beginning to think that's all you'll eat."

I didn't miss the way her eyes flashed when I said the word *we*. Even if Sullivan wasn't here right now, there was no mistaking that thoughts of him lingered. I wasn't the only man wooing her, and that was never too far from the back of my brain.

During dinner—Italian food this time—I learned

about her upbringing. Her strict, religious parents, an older sister, all who still lived in Texas. She spoke about them like she really missed them, and it was a feeling I couldn't really relate to. I had no family, no one back home who I felt guilty about not seeing enough.

"I'm actually overdue for a trip home. My mom is one of my best friends." Adrienne forked a piece of penne pasta, bringing it to her lips. She smiled as she chewed, looking lost in thought.

I wasn't really sure what to say. I had no family, other than Sullivan. But she was easy to talk to and the conversation flowed naturally between us. That was probably the best part—that nothing felt forced.

"Tell me about your date with Sullivan," I encouraged, wiping my mouth on my napkin.

Adrienne's eyes twinkled with something like a fond memory, and she smiled. "We had a really nice time. He's sweet. We fed baby ducklings."

I chuckled. "He's a good guy. I'm glad you had fun."

She nodded. "We did."

"And now, tonight…" I started, and her gaze latched

on to mine. "I know you said you wanted to go out with each of us separately. I would love to know what you're thinking. Is it what you imagined?"

At this, she folded her cloth napkin, and pushed her plate away. "I've had an amazing time today with you too, Will. I'm starting to understand this more now, starting to see that it'd be extremely difficult to choose between you."

Something inside me clenched. "We're not asking you to." In fact, that was the exact opposite of what I wanted.

Her brows knitted as though she was lost in thought, but a moment later, she gave a small nod of understanding. "I want you to know that I have no intention of coming between your friendship with Sullivan."

I felt the knot of tension begin to unravel. I sensed that she understood what Sullivan meant to me. Even without going into our history, or sharing our childhood, it seemed she was able to intuitively pick it up. Assuming we didn't scare her off, there would be time to go into all of that later.

We finished dinner, and I picked up the check, adding a generous gratuity before ushering her outside.

Back inside my SUV after our meal, I started the engine, then hesitated. I wasn't ready to drop her off at home, wasn't nearly ready to say goodnight.

She looked lost in thought, faraway. "What are you thinking?" I asked.

She shrugged. "It's just… I had a wonderful time, but…"

"But what?" I asked.

"When it's like this—one-on-one—I feel almost like I'm cheating on the other of you."

"You shouldn't." I placed my hand on her knee in a gesture I'd hoped would be calming, but the electricity snapping between us made that almost impossible. In the darkened interior of the car bathing us in moonlight, her faint feminine scent seducing me—I'd never wanted anything more.

My hand on her knee moved higher, stroking over her kneecap. Adrienne held her breath. "Sullivan and I don't keep secrets from each other. He told me how perfect you are—how tight and responsive. How quickly you came on his fingers last night."

A faint blush crept up her neck, but her eyes stayed on mine.

"I—Are you upset?" she asked, voice barely above a whisper.

I stroked her cheek with my thumb. "Not at all." Her skin was so smooth beneath my touch, and I stroked her cheek again. "You never have to worry about that— competition, jealousy, or anything like that between me and Sullivan. We learned how to share a long time ago."

Her lips formed into a slight smile and she nodded, but her eyes stayed guarded, like she wasn't completely convinced yet.

I continued, "That said, I have no idea what the lucky motherfucker did to play his cards right last night. And while I have zero expectations for how tonight will go, I know I'm not ready for you to leave. I know I need to kiss you."

I placed my hand on the back of her neck, guiding her closer, and when I leaned in, she met me halfway. Our kiss was firm, urgent, and Adrienne responded perfectly, bringing her hands to my chest and gripping the material of my shirt in her little fists. Her tongue swept out and met mine as I deepened the kiss. My cock gave a warning twitch beneath my zipper, as if to remind me he was there. Her tongue swirled perfectly with mine, and the chemistry between us I'd been wondering about threatened to explode.

Down, boy.

Adrienne made tiny whimpering sounds as her hands explored my muscled chest. It was fucking sexy.

When we finally broke apart, I traced my thumb along her lower lip. "Come back to our place for a bit?" I asked.

Adrienne nodded, and my cock hardened fully. "I suppose I could for a little while," she added.

Whether I wanted to be or not, I was all in. And when we arrived back home and were greeted by Sullivan, it was anyone's guess how far tonight would go.

Chapter Eight

Adrienne

SULLIVAN POURED ME A GLASS of wine in the kitchen and instructed me to go make myself more comfortable. Which is how I found myself sitting on the couch next to Will. But comfortable wasn't a word I'd use to describe my current state. Buzzed. Confused. Nervous. Turned on. Those were all much better adjectives.

I'd been out with Will and Sullivan three or four times now, but somehow I knew tonight would be different. Sweet kisses on the front porch before they dropped me off and sent me in to bed wouldn't be the extent of my night. I could sense it, could feel it in the air around us. The snapping of electricity. The pulse of sexual tension. It was bound to unravel. And soon. I just didn't know who would make the first move.

Sullivan joined us in the living room and handed me the glass of white wine. I accepted it and took a sip while he sat down on the other side of the couch—sandwiching me between them. I couldn't help but notice that neither of the men had a drink—yet I did. Something to calm my nerves, I supposed. With trembling fingers, I lifted the glass to my lips again and drank, more deeply this time, enjoying the crisp, sweet wine as it hit my tongue, and praying it would help relax me, because I'd never felt this keyed up in my entire life.

Will told Sullivan about our date, bragging about what a great shot I was, about the little Italian bistro with live music we enjoyed for dinner. But when the small talk was done and the silence settled around us, my stomach clenched with nerves.

"I'm sorry," I blurted, finally, unable to stand the silence any longer. I leaned forward to set my wineglass down on the coffee table but couldn't quite reach. Sullivan took it and placed it there for me.

"You have nothing to be sorry for," he soothed.

I was so on edge, I was almost ready to bolt—to leave now before I made a fool of myself. My hands were practically shaking. I drew a sharp inhale, trying to slow my ragged heartbeat. "This is just so far outside my comfort zone."

Sullivan moved closer to me on the couch. "Which means even more to us that you'd want to try. That you are here, with both of us."

Try. Wasn't that what I'd told myself? That I'd try it tonight—sort of as an experiment—and see how things went. But I already felt so confused and overwhelmed, I was ready to pull the plug on the entire evening. All that stuff I told Will on our date about my parents, about my family was true. I loved them with all my heart, we were extremely close-knit. But they were also very conservative in their beliefs, traditional through-and-through. They'd never accept me dating two men, and I'd never do anything to displease them.

But then Sullivan's hand came to rest on my jaw, his fingers lightly tracing my pulse, and all of my thoughts scattered in a million new directions. As he turned my face toward his, I was met by a dark, stormy gaze. He placed a soft, damp kiss on my lips, and then another. Slowly, I felt myself begin to relax.

"Nothing you can't handle, okay?" he murmured against my lips.

I nodded, my eyelids heavy. I felt drunk—but it wasn't the two swallows of wine I'd had—I was drunk on the lust I felt for these two, tempting men.

I wanted to know what Will thought about this—the man of few words—but instead, he stayed quiet, watching us, his gaze darkening as he did. It made my heart pound even faster to know he was watching us.

I placed one last kiss against Sullivan's lips, and then pulled back. "So how does it all work? Assuming I want to spend the night. Do you guys like flip a coin, or…"

At this, Will smiled and Sullivan let out a deep chuckle of laughter.

"No, sweetheart," Will said, moving closer to me on the couch, close enough that I could feel his body heat, smell his crisp, masculine cologne. Just having him near made my entire body clench in anticipation.

While I licked my lips and waited for a reply, Will and Sullivan locked eyes and seemed to engage in an unspoken conversation that happened above my head, within a few heartbeat's time. God, they were so sexy. So *infuriatingly* sexy.

"We've already discussed who will be the first inside you," Sullivan said.

Oh. This was news to me. My heartbeat hammered so fast and loud, I felt like I'd just run a marathon, or rather like I'd just sprinted the entire thing.

But rather than fill me in on what they had discussed, Sullivan leaned in close and pressed his lips to mine. While we kissed, I felt Will move closer, and his mouth began pressing damp kisses along the back of my neck. It sent shivers racing down my spine.

I wasn't sure what I had been expecting, but I had no idea it would feel like this. Two delicious-smelling, incredibly good-looking men kissing my lips, my neck, stroking my thighs, cupping my breasts... It was complete and total sensory overload. In the best way possible.

"Still unsure about how this will work?" Sullivan asked.

I opened my eyes, which now felt heavy.

Will turned my face toward his and pressed one more kiss to my mouth before I could answer.

"You want both of us, don't you?" he asked, stroking my cheek.

Both of them kissing and fondling me? It was like a gateway drug to ménage. And the bastards knew it.

"Yes," I said, voice sounding more confident than I

felt. I was flooded with so much sensation I could hardly form a coherent thought, much less put together an entire sentence.

Sullivan rose and offered me his hand. I let him help me up from the couch and lead me down the hall. Will followed and when we entered his bedroom, with its massive bed, the butterflies in my stomach came rushing back.

With the patience of saints, they undressed me, kissing and stroking each new inch of skin they exposed until I stood nearly bare between them, dressed only in a scrap of black lace that covered the needy spot between my legs.

"Jesus, you're beautiful," Will said, deep voice rasping over my skin like a soft caress. I felt more beautiful just then than I ever had before. With their lust-filled eyes appraising me, I felt like the most exquisite piece of priceless art. The feeling was addicting. Already, I didn't know how I'd ever go back to dating just one man at a time.

Sullivan bent down, sliding my panties down my legs, and Will supported my weight as Sullivan helped me step out of them. With a steadying hand on his arm, I met Will's eyes. They were so dark and stormy, so captivating that I couldn't look away. Sullivan turned me to face him, steering me by the shoulders.

"Relax," he murmured, lips on my neck. "Let us take care of you."

I gave a breathless response and his lips were back on mine. But not to be left out, Will's large palms glided over my skin, fingertips tracing soft, featherlight touches along my shoulders, arms, and back.

Suddenly, I wanted them every bit as exposed as I felt. Tugging at belt buckles, and fumbling with buttons, a feeling unlike anything I'd ever felt took hold. I pushed my hands into both of their jeans.

Having a cock in each one of my hands…it should have felt weird, right?

It didn't.

Not even a little.

I couldn't explain why, or what had come over me, but I wanted them both. Wanted to watch them lose control right along with me. Stroking each of them against my palm, I tested their weight.

"Off," I murmured. "Take them off." I sounded breathless, and slightly out of control.

Scratch that, a whole lot out of control.

Will and Sullivan stopped kissing and caressing me long enough to pull their shirts off over their heads, and then jeans and boxers were pushed off and kicked out of the way.

My throat felt tight and completely dry. I couldn't have formed a single, coherent thought if I tried.

Because holy fuck.

The carnal feast of skin and muscle and male flesh before me was completely overwhelming.

Will was solid muscle from head to toe, with a patch of trimmed hair on his chest, and a thick erection that pointed up to the sky. Not to be outdone, Sullivan, the trimmer of the two, was nicely toned and with a six-pack of his own. His erection wasn't quite as thick, but it was longer, reaching almost all the way up to his belly button.

I only had time to suck in a ragged inhale, and both men were on me again, kissing and stroking, and looking at me with wonder. Sullivan nuzzled against my breasts, his mouth leaving damp, sucking kisses all along my skin. Will cradled my jaw in his large hands, kissing me slowly, and deeply while watching my reactions. I couldn't help but feel this was some kind of test.

Were they waiting for me to freak out? To call the whole thing off?

My hands seemed to have a mind of their own, finding each man's hard length and giving a languid stroke up, and then back down as I adjusted to the size and feel of them in my fists.

They were each so different, Sullivan shuddering like he was sensitive to my touch, and Will remaining stock-still, except for the leaking, little white drop on his tip.

Will pressed his lips to my neck, whispering, "There's something incredibly sexy about a woman who can handle two men at the same time."

A hot shiver raced down my spine. I didn't know this woman—hadn't known this side of myself even existed.

Will and Sullivan locked eyes for a moment and I wished I could tell what they were thinking in that moment.

Things between the men didn't seem at all strange,

which was somewhat surprising given that we were all naked. But it made me happy to know they weren't going to act weird or self-conscious. I had to keep reminding myself that this was their normal, even if it was totally outside my comfort zone.

Sullivan's teeth grazed my nipple as he bit down playfully, and I let out a little yelp.

Suddenly overwhelmed by everything that was happening so quickly, I swayed on my feet. And then someone was lifting me, carrying me over to the bed where I was placed carefully in the center.

The size of Will's bed seemed to defy logic. I expected more awkward positioning, more jockeying for a spot, but there was none of that. There was just mouths moving, and tongues exploring, and fingers stroking, and oh my God—my body racing toward orgasm much faster than I ever expected.

It felt like the sexual equivalent of winning a game of roulette in Las Vegas, my body was all flashing lights and DINGDINGDINGS. I was all kinds of lit up, and walking away now simply was not an option. Common sense ceased to exist, all the warnings Dani cautioned me about—poof, gone.

Sullivan kissed a path down my belly and positioned himself between my legs, lapping at me eagerly while Will's deep, drugging kisses drowned out my cries of pleasure. Will took my hand in his, kissing my knuckles, and then placed it around his cock, where he used my hand to jack himself off. It was the most erotic thing I'd ever seen. He kissed me, and nipped at my lips, and worked my hand up and down while I thrust a hand into Sullivan's hair, my hips squirming.

Sullivan's tongue seemed to know the exact pace, the pressure I needed and moved with such precision. A few moments later, and he quickly brought me to orgasm with his mouth. My body pulsed with pleasure as the intense climax washed through me.

With my heartbeat pounding in my throat, I barely had time to recover before Sullivan was moving to lie beside me. With one man on each side of me, I felt so cherished and adored. Their attention was dizzying.

"An Adrienne sandwich," Sullivan said, smiling at me.

"My favorite kind," Will murmured, lips at my throat again.

I wasn't quite sure what to do next, but then Will's hand traveled down my belly while Sullivan stroked my skin lightly with the pads of his fingers.

"Can you come again?" Sullivan asked.

He was asking if I could come for Will.

Despite having just reached a climax, my body begged for more.

"Yes…" I whispered. I actually didn't know for sure—I wasn't a multiples type of girl, but I wanted to. For him. For them.

Will knew exactly what he was doing, his fingers moving slowly at first, seeking out all the secret spots that made me tremble, before gaining confidence in what I liked best.

A sexy, low growl tumbled from Will's parted lips as he watched my reactions to his touch.

Unrelenting in his pursuit for my pleasure, his strokes shook me to my very core, body trembling, breasts bouncing with each firm thrust of his fingers inside me.

Sullivan's large palm rested on my belly, admiring, watching as Will brought me to orgasm for a second time, using only his hand. The climax tore through me, leaving me breathless, panting, and trembling from head to toe.

Drunk off the endorphins from a second powerful release, I was so boneless and sated that at first, I didn't even notice that both men were lying on either side of me yet again. When I was able to finally focus, I could see them communicating with an unspoken glance, the eye contact between them lasting several seconds as they seemed to make a game plan for what happened next.

Will took my hand again, kissed the palm and placed it on his thick cock. Then Sullivan took my other hand and did the same, intertwining our fingers around his long, hot shaft.

If I'd felt any pressure to perform before, that was all gone. Each man showed me what he liked—the speed, the tempo, the grip strength, everything.

Will liked a firm grip, and short, even strokes.

Sullivan preferred a looser grip that allowed for long, deep pulls from his base all the way to the broad tip.

My nipples pebbled into hard knots as my hands continued to work. If I expected this moment to be filled with imbalance, asymmetry, I couldn't have been more wrong. Turning my face to kiss Will, and then to the other side to kiss Sullivan, I found it wasn't as difficult as I imagined it would be to divide my attention. I just did what came naturally.

"Fuck," Will cursed, under his breath. "That feels incredible." His abdominal muscles flexed and clenched as his breathing grew more ragged.

"I'm close," Sullivan grunted.

He said it almost more to Will than he did to me, and I wondered if they had some unspoken agreement about timing their releases close together or something.

Then, a few moments later, Will cursed again, his free hand tangling in my hair as he brought my mouth to his. A warm, sticky drizzle of come lubricated my final strokes as his body shuddered.

"Fuck, sweetheart. So good," he groaned out, lips still against mine.

Sullivan made a soft noise of pleasure, and I turned my attention to him. His hand fell away, but I knew what he liked by now, and after a few more firm strokes, he murmured my name, as he came all over my hand and his stomach.

A few more kisses, and then I was being carried into the bathroom, and placed before the sink where I washed my hands. And then it was back to the bed where Sullivan laid me against a pile of pillows, and Will drew a fuzzy throw blanket over me.

We cuddled there together, kissing and talking for a long time. I didn't want to let on, but what I'd just experienced had shaken me to my very core. It was complete and total sexual gratification unlike anything I'd ever experienced.

And I didn't see how I'd ever go back.

Chapter Nine

Sullivan

"DAMN, THAT LOOKS PRETTY." I ran my hand over the marble countertop my contractor had just finished installing. The pale stone contrasted nicely with the dark cabinets I'd installed myself last week.

All day at work, my thoughts kept wandering back to last night. And every time I did, my boxers felt two sizes too small.

"Glad you like it, boss," José said, grabbing his caulking gun and shoving it into his tool belt.

José gathered his tools, ready to head out for the day.

"You need anything else?" he asked over one shoulder as he caught me, lost deep in thought yet again.

"We're good. Have a good night."

He nodded. "See you in the morning."

José left, leaving me in the half-finished home alone. The silence of a home without electricity or running water is a silence like no other. I didn't particularly care for the dead silence. Never had.

It reminded me too much of growing up in the orphanage. It was so lonely and quiet, not filled with any life, well, not until the year I turned ten, and Will moved in to the home I was staying in. Everything changed that year. His presence was almost larger than life—and suddenly things went from boring and lonely to exciting. We played pick-up basketball games in the park, went fishing in the creek, played hooky from school, and spent afternoons just walking around town, going to the park or doing nothing at all.

Life was so much simpler back then. But these days, life was pretty damn good, too. I had a thriving business, and if last night was any indication, the possibility for a romantic relationship with Adrienne.

Last night couldn't have gone any better if I'd scripted it ahead of time.

Leaning one hip against the counter, I ran my hand over the smooth, cool surface, smiling as I remembered it in vivid detail. The sated look on Adrienne's pretty, heart-shaped face after she'd come—twice. She was so limp, and almost sleepy, as Will and I took control…showing her how to take care of us both when she was too far gone to expend much energy. It made me even more eager to do it again. We'd have to work up to more, go easy on her if we both wanted to fuck her, especially in the same night. And I knew we did.

Surveying the kitchen a final time, I felt satisfied with the progress. Time to get out of here and head home. It was almost dinnertime as my stomach reminded me. And I had something important I wanted to discuss with Will tonight.

I grabbed my cell phone and keys from the windowsill and made my way to the back door where I locked up and dialed Will.

"Hey," I said when he answered.

"You done for the day?" he asked.

"Yep. Headed home. It's my night to cook, right?"

He grunted something that sounded like a yes.

"What are you doing?" I asked, sliding into my truck and starting the engine.

"Grabbing a quick workout."

I glanced at the clock. Twenty minutes until I got

home, thirty if I stopped at the store, like I needed to. Which meant he'd probably be in the shower when I got home. Will had always been a fitness-fanatic, but he seemed to work out more now than ever since we'd finished our home gym.

"And, yeah. Your night to cook," he said around another grunt.

I shook my head, smiling as I pictured him probably shirtless and sweating his ass off. He probably had the air conditioning cranked down to an ungodly level, too.

"Alright. I'm going to stop by the store. Steaks or barbequed chicken?"

"Surprise me," he said.

I chuckled. "Will do."

I clicked off the phone and turned out onto the main road.

Our relationship was so uncomplicated, so blissfully perfect that sometimes I couldn't quite believe my luck. I didn't know what I'd done to deserve a best friend like Will. Actually, best friend was entirely the wrong word. He was family. The kind of family you chose. Which made tonight's conversation even more tricky. The last thing I wanted to do was upset him. But there was something I needed to get off my chest, and it wasn't something I could decide on my own.

Chapter Ten

Adrienne

"JUST HEAR US OUT," Sullivan started, his voice soft.

Will looked down at his hands and my stomach twisted itself into an intricate knot. *Ugh.*

The use of the word *us* didn't quite seem to fit. Sullivan was the one doing all the talking, and I couldn't help but wonder about Will's opinion on the topic. Was he even on the same page?

Something inside me needed to know.

"Will?" I asked.

His dark eyes raised to mine. "Yeah, sweetheart?"

I licked my lips and took a deep breath.

I was seated on a stool at their kitchen island, a glass of wine sitting before me. A tray of cheese, crackers, and fruit untouched nearby, and both men hovered in the center of the kitchen. Sullivan leaning one hip against the counter, and Will standing farther away, beside the stove.

My eyes met Will's dark gaze. "Is this ... what you

want?" Moments ago, Sullivan proposed that I move in, and an awful, all-encompassing silence stretched between us, sucking out all the oxygen in the room. Before I could even decide what I wanted, I needed to know that they were both on the same page, and Will was being quiet.

My heart pounded dully against my ribcage.

"It's a bit soon, but, fuck, I'm not opposed to it. Not at all," Will finished, scrubbing one hand over the back of his neck.

I swallowed and nodded. "Yeah. I feel the exact same way. It's soon, but … " I laughed, a chuckle that came out more nervous-sounding than I thought it would. "I have to admit, I don't hate the idea."

Maybe it was because after a week and a half, I already felt like I'd overstayed my welcome with Dani. And because I was so damn tired of sleeping on that hard-as-a-rock couch of hers. And because these men were just … so hard to say no to.

"It's the perfect idea. And it's just temporary," Sullivan said, encouragingly. "There's no need to overthink this. Just until your place is finished."

I glanced toward Will again, and he gave a subtle

nod. "Say yes, sweetheart."

It was only two more weeks, at most, until my apartment was ready. And even though I really didn't want to over-wear my welcome with Dani, this was crazy. I hardly knew them. A handful of dates, one intimate encounter, and now they were asking me to move in? This was all so fast, yet it felt totally normal. *What was wrong with me?*

"Just until my apartment is done," I said.

Sullivan's mouth lifted in a smile, and Will's posture relaxed like this pleased him.

"The moment you get uncomfortable, the moment this isn't working for you …" Sullivan began, and then Will held up one hand.

Will's dark eyes roamed mine. "Stay for dinner."

I nodded. "Yes." I was saying yes to both of their requests.

Sullivan broke into a happy smile and straightened his posture. "Perfect. I already sent someone over to pick up your bags. We'll have dinner and figure the rest out as we go."

Will nodded and reached for me.

I took his hand, and when he tugged me close I folded myself in against his broad chest, and relished in his warm, masculine embrace.

Sullivan patted my ass with a smile, and then turned back to the stove where a pot of chicken soup simmered.

I had to admit, to be here was much more relaxing than at Dani's. This home was beautiful, organized, and calm. There were no worried or judgmental stares, no crying babies…

After a casual dinner of creamy chicken soup and warm bread fresh from the oven, Will, Sullivan, and I retired to the couch in the living room. My bags had arrived an hour ago and were currently sitting untouched in the hallway. I had no idea what happened next, whose bedroom I was supposed to sleep in, or what would take place later. The darker it grew outside, the more confused I became about how the evening would unfold.

I clutched the stem of my wineglass and swallowed the last sip.

"Adrienne … we want you to make yourself at home," Sullivan said, placing one large hand against my shoulder and giving it a squeeze.

"I could run you a bath. Would that relax you?" Will asked.

The surprising sweetness from Will was unexpected. I nodded my head. "A bath sounds nice."

He had a huge, freestanding tub in his master bathroom, so it wasn't surprising when he grabbed my bags and wandered into his bedroom, and then into the adjoining master bath. I wondered if that had answered the question about whose bed I would stay in tonight.

Sullivan didn't say a word, but rose from the couch to rinse my empty wineglass in the kitchen sink as I followed Will into the bathroom.

Warm water filled the tub and Will set a container of Epsom salts on the edge of the tub. "How hot do you like it?"

"Hot," I confirmed.

This earned me a rare smile from him, and I felt my belly flip.

I began stripping out of my jeans and t-shirt, and rather than stay and ogle me, Will ducked out of the bathroom, closing the door firmly behind him.

Fixing my long hair up into a messy bun, I slipped into the hot water, shutting the faucet off with my toe once it was filled to my liking. It felt incredible and I let out a long exhale.

I could hear the low murmur of men's voices from the other room, and as much as I wanted to strain to hear what it was that they were discussing, since I very well may be the topic of the hour, part of me was glad that I couldn't quite hear. It wasn't any of my business what they discussed.

That night I slept in Will's bed, but aside from a lingering good night kiss, he didn't lay a finger on me.

The next two days passed that way. We woke early, fixing coffee, and showering before rushing off to work, only to come home to each other at night, lingering over dinner and sometimes a glass of wine for me and Sullivan. I learned Will rarely drank. I learned he also had a hard time sleeping. I wasn't sure if my presence helped him or interfered with his sleeping patterns, but I'd woken in the night more than once to feel him tossing and turning.

I wasn't sure if I should split my time equally and opt

to sleep in Sullivan's bed tonight. But true to their word, there was no jealousy or awkward territorial displays between them, and for that I was grateful. I was still getting my footing being part of this threesome.

It was my third day staying with them, and I'd woken early, and had already showered, dressed and blow-dried my hair by the time the men came ambling from their respective bedrooms.

"Morning, sweetheart," Will said, giving my backside a squeeze as he passed by me in the kitchen. He looked like he'd already showered, with slightly damp hair, dressed in jeans and a t-shirt.

Sullivan followed behind him, wrapping his arms around me from the back, and nuzzling in against my neck. "Mmm, you smell good," he said, placing a kiss against the back of my neck.

"Thank you." I wrapped my hands around my coffee mug, and went to sit at the kitchen island, intent to observe them as they moved about the kitchen.

Already I knew little things about them, like how they liked to start their day. Sullivan usually made himself two scrambled eggs, while Will preferred only coffee—which he drank black. I'd long ago grown accustomed to grabbing breakfast at the café by work with my friend and stylist, Tyler. Usually a scone or muffin did the trick to hold me over until lunch.

Will poured himself a mug of coffee, but the moment he took a sip, I knew something was very wrong. Standing over the sink, he spat the coffee down the drain.

"What the hell was that?" he asked, brows pinched together.

"Um, coffee?" I offered.

He shook his head, before rinsing his mouth with water. "That wasn't coffee."

I held up the bag of caramel mocha flavored coffee I'd bought last night and brewed this morning. I could have laughed if his expression wasn't so serious. He looked like someone pissed in his mug.

"Don't be mad," I said, offering him a slight smile. "It's flavored."

He stalked closer, caging himself in between where my legs dangled from the barstool, his large palm caressing my cheek. "Do I look mad?"

I shook my head.

He pressed a kiss to my mouth. "Just warn a guy next time."

"Noted." I chuckled, warmly.

His hand fell away from my cheek, and he took a step back, and his eyes were still on mine, even as he directed his question to Sullivan. "I'm going to head over to the flooring manufacturer. Plans set for tonight?"

Sullivan nodded a brief yes before cracking two eggs into a pan. I wasn't sure what plans they meant, but I was eager to find out. Especially since I had a strange feeling these plans most definitely involved me.

***

Later, I was folding a load of my laundry when my cell phone rang from the other room. Folding a pair of leggings and setting them aside, I jogged for the living room and grabbed my phone from the couch.

"Hey, Dani," I said after checking the caller ID.

"Hey." Her voice was uncharacteristically high. "I just wanted to check on you. Still alive?"

I chuckled. A little better than that, actually, but I

didn't want to brag. I had two doting new boyfriends and honestly, sometimes it felt a little unfair. It felt like I'd hit the jackpot, and I was afraid of making other people jealous with my good fortune.

"Doing just fine," I said, wandering back to the laundry room to finish folding. "I have the rest of the afternoon off, and the guys are still at work."

"Good." She sounded truly relieved.

"And how about you guys? How's Bella? Are you getting enough sleep yet?" It felt like I'd been gone much longer than three days.

"Yes, thank God. Bella's finally sleeping six hours at a time at night. It's heaven."

I smiled into the phone. "Oh, that's amazing."

Dani grew quiet for a minute, but I waited her out, knowing there was something on her mind. She wasn't the talk-on-the-phone type, she almost always texted. My patience was rewarded a few seconds later.

"So…spill it, girl. What's it like with two men?"

"What do you mean? It's the same as being with one man, except there are two of them."

She laughed. "I meant the sex. Give me the details. Is it good? Weird? *Crazy?*"

I rolled my eyes and folded the last tank top, adding it to the top of the pile. "Actually, I wouldn't know."

After a beat of silence, she exhaled. "What the hell does that mean?" her voice was filled with surprise.

I swallowed. "We've messed around, but we haven't gone all the way yet…" My voice came out quieter than I intended. "I guess they're wanting to take it slow."

It was surprising to me, too. I had no idea what they were waiting for. Maybe they just weren't feeling it. Weren't feeling me…but that didn't make sense either. They'd been so devoted, so sweet, and attentive. I could see their attraction to me in their lingering glances, their sweet hugs and kisses.

"Maybe they wanted to make sure you weren't going to run. They said they don't do casual, right?"

"Right." That was the word I said, but the words I was thinking could have filled an entire page. Were they waiting, deliberately, because they were worried their brand of love-making would scare me off? Were they into some kinky stuff? Well, kinkier than a threesome inherently was…

Before I could respond, my phone beeped, indicating that I had another call. "One second, Dani. I'll be right back."

It was Sullivan, and in a few brief sentences, he had my heart pounding out an erratic rhythm in my chest. After we were through, I clicked back over to Dani.

"That was Sullivan."

"And?" she asked, voice inquisitive.

"He said to get ready, that they're taking me on a nice date tonight."

Dani made a squeal of excitement. "Oh my God, tonight's the night, then. Wear your good panties. And a matching bra. And don't forget to shave."

My stomach twisted with nerves. Okay, then. *Game on.*

"I've got to run, Dani. I need to go get ready."

"Roger that. Good luck with the … double penetration." She laughed and my stomach tightened even further.

Awesome.

I had no idea what tonight would entail, only that it was certain to change everything going forward.

Chapter Eleven

Sullivan

I TOSSED THE VALET THE KEYS to my SUV, and wandered around the front to meet Adrienne, only to find that Will was already standing beside her with his hand curled protectively around her waist.

A spark of heat zipped down my spine, pooling low. I liked seeing them together. His masculinity—her feminine curves…there was something about it that was so damn pleasing to me.

She turned her head to me, and leaned in close, pressing a kiss to my cheek. Flanking her on either side, we escorted her into the restaurant as the hostess and valet both gawked, open-mouthed at us.

It was something I was used to, but Adrienne, not so much. She ducked her chin to her chest, looking down at the sexy pair of high heels she'd worn.

"Hey." I lifted her chin toward mine. "Don't. We have nothing to be ashamed of."

Wide, blue eyes latched onto mine, and she gave a

determined nod, but her lips were still pressed tight.

We followed the hostess to a table at the back of the restaurant with large windows overlooking the twinkling lights of the city beyond. It was perfect, quiet, and out of the way.

As Will helped her into her chair, I sat down across from her, leaving him to take the open spot beside her.

Nerves danced in my stomach as her eyes flitted up to meet mine, a secret smile on her lips. Tonight was the night. We all knew that. It was buzzing like an electric current between us even now. I took a deep breath and picked up my menu while Adrienne and Will did the same.

"Wine tonight?" Adrienne asked.

"Absolutely," I said. "Should I pick us a bottle?"

"Please," she murmured.

I knew she liked crisp, fruity whites. I also knew that Will would drive us home so she and I could indulge. But I didn't want to indulge too much, I needed to be clear-headed tonight. I knew that Will was thinking the same thing, I knew him well enough to know he wouldn't order anything too heavy, and that he'd skip dessert.

The waitress came by, and after I ordered a bottle of wine, Will requested a glass of club soda with lime. The drinks were delivered to our table quickly, and I couldn't help but notice our waitress seemed a little too eager, hovering around us like she was trying to solve some great mystery. I only hoped Adrienne didn't really notice. I didn't want her to have any added stress tonight. After we'd placed our orders, Adrienne smiled and lifted her wineglass to her lips for a long swallow.

"So…" she started,

She was adorably nervous.

"Tell us," I said.

Her brows scrunched together. "Tell you what?"

Will's eyes danced knowingly on mine.

I licked my lips and leaned in closer. "What your reservations are."

"My…?" She hesitated, taking another sip of her wine to buy herself some time.

"What your hang-ups are about this," Will added as his hand pointed between him and myself.

Adrienne blinked twice, taking in our words. "My

hang-ups? This week, you guys haven't even so much as laid a finger on me." Her cheeks flushed slightly, and she leaned closer, lowering her voice. "You didn't…"

"We were waiting for you," Will explained.

Her blue gaze snapped up to his. "Waiting for me? That makes no sense."

I set down my wineglass and reached for her hand. "We wanted to give you the time you needed to work this out. Time to accept it all. We know it's a lot to process."

Will took her other hand, lacing his fingers between hers. "We didn't want to do anything until we were certain you were ready."

She pressed her full lips together, considering it. "Oh."

When the waitress came by to deliver our food, Adrienne tugged her hands from ours, stuffing them under the table where she fiddled with her napkin.

With flushed cheeks, like she knew she'd just interrupted something, the waitress set a plate in front of each one of us in silence, before scuttling away again.

"So, you were waiting for me to make the first

move?" Adrienne asked, voice low.

Will shook his head, correcting her. "Not the first move, no. A sign."

"A sign?" she asked.

"Like not holding our hands in public…that's a sign you're not ready for this. We didn't want to rush you."

Her shoulders relaxed like she understood my meaning for the first time. It would take some time for her to get used to the new dynamic of this relationship. I accepted that, and I was a patient man. I meant what I said about not rushing her.

"I wish I could tell you it's something that goes away, that the way the valet, hostess, and waitress looked at us were just isolated events. But I won't lie to you. This won't be easy. There will always be questions, there will always be people who don't understand."

Will placed his hand on my shoulder and gave it a reassuring squeeze. His touch always seemed to calm me.

I took a deep breath, and continued, "But I also promise you that it'll be worth it. If you open yourself up to this, it can be amazing."

Adrienne smiled shyly, and reached for my hand first, and then Will's. She gave our hands a reassuring squeeze, no longer caring who saw. "I understand. And I promise to try."

I bought her hand to my lips and kissed the back of it. "That's all we're asking for."

Will smiled, and when his eyes met mine a thousand words were exchanged in one heartbeat's time. We'd cleared the air, but what happened later would be anyone's guess.

"Now, let's eat," I said.

I focused on my food, watching Adrienne from the corner of my eye. She took another sip of wine, and then forked a bite of chicken, bringing it to her lips.

The waitress hovered again, this time checking to see if we needed anything else, and Will let out a deep chuckle, making all of us smile.

"You know she's only jealous," I said, once the waitress was gone.

"She'd give anything to be in your shoes right now," Will added.

Adrienne's lips tipped up into a smile. "I don't know. These shoes are pretty uncomfortable."

"Smartass," Will muttered under his breath.

With a promise to rub her feet later, and with the unspoken promise of so much more, we dug in and enjoyed our dinner.

***

With his hands gripping her waist, Will pushed through the front door, and hastily pressed Adrienne's back against the wall in the foyer. He devoured her neck with kisses while she writhed, her hazy, half-lidded eyes finding mine. I closed the door and moved farther inside. Watching him lose control, seeing her come undone in his arms…my cock gave an eager twitch, but rather than join them just yet, I leaned back against the opposite wall, feeling happily voyeuristic, and a whole lot turned on.

Pushing his hand into her panties, I knew the second Will's fingers found her wet, because he released a soft grunt of need. That sound sent my heart ricocheting faster. Adrienne let out a little whimper of frustration, and her head dropped back against the wall with a dull thud. She gripped his biceps, holding on as he began the slow dance of readying her for us.

Or hell, maybe he was just teasing her, because the line creasing her forehead stayed where it was.

"Sull…" Adrienne reached for me, and my heart quickened with the knowledge that she needed me near. When I stepped closer, her hand dropped to the eager erection inside my jeans, rubbing me through the fabric.

Her expression relaxed as we caged her in against the wall, one muscular body on each side of her.

"Ride his fingers," I whispered against the side of her neck.

I felt her shiver against me.

Will's eyes were dark with lust as he began to fuck her in earnest with his fingers, while she grinded on his with as much intensity as he was giving.

I took her mouth, kissing her deeply, which did nothing to tamper her desperate moans.

"She's getting close," Will said, voice ragged.

"Don't come yet," I warned.

"But…"

I shushed her with another kiss. "Not." *Kiss.* "Yet."

"Where?" she gasped.

"Bedroom," I managed.

"Whose?" Her cheeks were flushed, her eyes half-lidded.

"Mine," Will barked.

In a tangle of limbs, we fell onto Will's bed, and then he and I rose on our knees in a wordless agreement to strip her naked. Each new creamy inch of skin we exposed made my cock ache. She was so perfect. Soft, and pale, with curves where a woman ought to have curves. I wanted to kiss every soft inch of flesh, but forced myself to slow down. To appreciate this moment. When I trailed the back of my knuckles along her belly, she sucked in a breath.

Will's hand slid down her calf as he brought one slender foot to his lips and placed a kiss against the arch. Her pink-painted toes curled as she shifted on the bed.

"How?" she panted.

I shook my head. "That's for us to worry about. Just lie back and relax."

And with a combined look of sheer ecstasy and an 'easier said than done' expression, Adrienne looked at us both, all the while realizing in that moment that she held every ounce of power over this situation. "I trust you both."

Chapter Twelve

Adrienne

I WAS TRYING to do what Sullivan asked. Trying like hell to lie back and relax, but my heart was pounding so hard and fast, and my hips seemed to have a mind of their own, lifting to seek friction as Will moved between my thighs.

Tugging his shirt off over his head, my hands explored every valley and ridge of muscle in his sexy chest.

Then he pushed his boxer briefs down, freeing himself, and gripped his wide length, rubbing himself up and down over me. The sensation shot through me with such force, it stole my breath, and a wild plea tumbled from my lips.

Sullivan tossed a condom at Will, but rather than catch it, he let it drop to the bed beside my thigh.

Their eyes met, and for a few moments, nobody said a word. My pulse thundered in my ears, drowning out everything else. *Was something wrong?*

"I'm on birth control," I said finally. "And I'm clean. But I don't want to take any chances, if you guys aren't …"

"We're sure," Will finished for them both.

And then Will was aligning himself at my center and steadying my hips as he thrust inside so exquisitely slowly.

My breath left my lungs in a harsh pant, and the pressure of him stretching me made my eyes squeeze closed.

"Slow," Sullivan said to him, his voice a warning.

Apparently they'd decided that Will would be the first inside me, but that didn't seem to stop Sullivan from having opinions about how it was done. If I'd been able to think clearly, I would have made some joke about him being a backseat driver. But I could barely formulate a coherent response, much less a humorous one.

Because all logical thought had fled. I opened my eyes and watched as the strong, sexy Will bit down on his lip with a look of determination. So hot. He felt so good. And then Sullivan brought his hand to my belly, sliding lower until his fingers moved down to circle my clit.

Will's hips began pumping, testing my limits, and

Sullivan teased my wet flesh with gentle touches. The moment was so unexpectedly erotic—I realized right then that four hands were much better than two. And two mouths were quite simply indescribable. Will's mouth was on my breasts, sucking and nipping while Sullivan kissed me deeply. It was only a matter of minutes before I was coming apart at the seams, moaning and arching, and climaxing wildly as Will stayed buried deep inside.

Holy hell!

Sullivan and Will traded positions, and for a moment, I almost protested, but then Will placed a soft kiss on my mouth, quieting me. As Sullivan settled himself between my thighs, and Will laid down beside me, I noticed it was almost like they were careful not to actually touch each other during sex, despite how comfortable they seemed together. Something about that seemed off to me and I couldn't quite put my finger on what, but they'd made it very clear all along that this was about me and my pleasure so that had to be part of it.

And then Sullivan was parting my legs, gripping himself in one hand and pressing into me. My eyes nearly rolled back in my head.

"Fuck, baby," he groaned, burying himself so deep I saw stars. Being with them like this was so insanely arousing, that I found myself breathing in shuddering, shaky gasps, tiny whimpers falling from my parted lips.

Will's large palm rested on my cheek, turning my face toward his. "You okay?" he asked, his voice uncharacteristically tender.

I gave a tight nod, and we kissed, tongues tangling as I fought to hold in the moans from Sullivan pounding into me.

"You felt so good coming on my cock," Will murmured against my lips.

My eyes opened and latched onto his. I reached for him, touching any bare patch of skin I could reach.

"I don't want to leave you out," I said. He hadn't come yet, a fact I was acutely aware of despite how out of it I felt.

Without a word, he guided my hand to his mouth, wetting my palm with his saliva before bringing it to his swollen shaft. I pumped him in quick strokes.

I sensed Sullivan watching us, and the idea of him watching me pleasure Will sent a hot pulse of need racing through me. My body clenched around Sullivan and he let out a curse.

"Fuck," Sullivan growled. "Gonna come already."

My gaze met his. "Me too."

It was all the encouragement he needed, because then he was growling and tensing, and coming apart inside me. And I followed right behind him, a second powerful release tearing through me with such ferocity that I almost passed out. It seemed to go on and on until my entire body, from the top of my head to the tip of my toes, felt tingly.

Will let out a ragged exhale as my hand continued working him over.

I felt almost dizzy with the knowledge that I was the one making these men lose their minds in pleasure. Me. The girl who'd struggled to find one man now suddenly had two.

Once Sullivan had finished, he carefully eased out, and Will wasted no time in tugging my limp body over and on top of his. With his hot length pressed between us, Will began thrusting and grinding his cock against me, the wetness between my legs aiding him.

"You're perfect," he moaned, mouth against my neck. One hand roamed to my ass and brushed against the sensitive spot between my cheeks. "Has anyone ever taken you here, Adrienne?"

I shuttered. "N-no." Before I could process his question further, Will grunted my name, and then he was tangling his hands in my hair and climaxing with a groan.

Chapter Thirteen

Sullivan

AFTER HELPING ADRIENNE into the bathroom where we all washed up, Will and I carried her back to bed. He tossed her into the center of it and she let out a squeal. Her eyes were bright and her expression happy.

Cuddling beside her, I drew the blankets over us. Will slipped into a pair of boxer briefs and joined us, lying down on the other side of her.

"Wow. That was ..." Adrienne began, and then let out a soft giggle, her hand coming up to cover her mouth like she was embarrassed by her reaction.

Will and I exchanged a look. We were familiar with this—the total sexual gratification that the two of us together were able to provide. The dreamy look in a woman's eyes the first time she experienced ménage, the almost reverent haze it left you in. It was what came after today that would define our relationship, that would determine if it all worked out. But right now the mood surrounding us was light, playful, and I was determined to enjoy it.

"Did you enjoy yourself, sweetheart?" Will asked. His voice was soft, sleepy. It was crazy how his mood morphed into something so tender after he came. *Typical male.* I smirked to myself as I watched them together. He tucked her hair behind her ear and stared down at her in wonder.

"It was … incredible. Better than anything." She placed her hand on his cheek, and then laced her free hand with mine. "You were both…"

"We know." I smirked at her.

Adrienne rolled her eyes, her mouth breaking into a happy grin. "Cocky, much?"

I shrugged. "It's not cocky if it's true."

Will reached over and chucked a pillow at my head. "Less talking, more cuddling." He tugged Adrienne closer to him, tucking her in against his side.

"So bossy," I murmured, spooning myself around Adrienne's backside.

She felt so nice, so soft and curvy and warm. I could stay just like this forever.

Generally after sex, we'd retreat to our own beds. It

had never been a problem before. And during Adrienne's first few nights here, we'd let her take the lead in deciding whose bed she'd share. But after what we'd shared tonight, there was no way I was going back to my bed alone.

Will cracked one eye open and glanced at me. "You're not sleeping naked in my bed, dude."

I rolled my eyes, but I couldn't help but smile. He wasn't asking me to leave. With an exhale, I rose from the bed and tugged on a pair of boxer briefs from Will's dresser before climbing back in beneath the sheets. "Happy now?"

"Did you just put on my underwear?" he asked.

Adrienne chuckled between us, her body quaking in laughter, even as her eyes stayed closed.

I didn't point out that when we were fucking our girl my cock was mere inches away from his at any given time. Yet it was the thought of me wearing his boxers that made him raise an eyebrow?

"I wanted clean boxers to sleep in. Relax. They'll be in the washing machine tomorrow."

He grunted something that sounded like acceptance and that was the end of it.

"'Night, baby," I whispered into the back of Adrienne's neck. She made a sleepy sound of comfort, tucked warmly between me and Will.

Soon, their breathing became deep and even and I knew they were both asleep. I wasn't sure if sleep was slower to come because I was unaccustomed to sleeping in Will's bed, or if it was because I simply had a lot on my mind. In only a matter of weeks, I was already falling for the woman nestled between us. And despite all my bravado to Will, all my confidence about her and us— now that real feelings were on the line, I couldn't help but wonder if this was all just in passing fun for her. A brief stint on the wild side, something to try, the chance to tick ménage à trois off her bucket list.

It wasn't a thought that sat well with me. The longer I laid there in silence, one lone question swirled through my brain, and for now, it was one without an answer.

Could she ever truly love both of us?

Chapter Fourteen

Adrienne

IT WAS A LONG DAY at work, and as the remaining traces of hair were swept from the floor, and the cash register was closed out, I finally let out a deep sigh.

Tyler, my friend and one of my best stylists, walked by and patted my shoulder. "You alright, girl?"

I nodded absently. "Just tired. Today was crazy."

Tyler nodded. "Fact."

It was a Saturday, which was always one of our busiest days in the salon, but today we had two different wedding parties complete with bridal parties, mothers-in-law and two rather demanding brides. My feet were killing me, and I was starving.

"Any plans tonight?" Tyler asked, checking his reflection in the full-length mirror as we headed toward the door. I always appreciated the evenings he closed with me. He was so efficient and cheery, we got through the whole routine fast enough to be out within thirty minutes of the last guest leaving. It wasn't even dark outside yet.

I let out a yawn and shook my head. "Sullivan texted earlier. I think we're just going to have a quiet dinner at home. Maybe watch a movie."

Tyler cocked an eyebrow at me. " Dinner, a movie, and then a threesome. Yes, you live such a domestic and boring life."

I shook my head, a smirk curling on my lips. "Hush. I'm starting to regret telling you about Will and Sullivan at all."

"Lies. You love my commentary." Tyler flipped off the lights and held open the front door for me. "After you."

I fished my keys out from the bottom of my purse and locked the front door before we hugged goodbye, each heading toward our cars in the parking lot.

"'Night, girl!" he called over one shoulder as he strutted toward his car—a lime green convertible that fit his fun, quirky personality perfectly.

"'Night, Ty!" I called back.

Fifteen minutes later I arrived home and parked my car behind Sullivan's truck. It looked like Will wasn't home yet. It was crazy how comfortable I'd become at their place in only a couple weeks' time. Now, my apartment was almost done, but I couldn't really imagine going home alone to the lonely space I'd once loved.

Inside, I found Sullivan humming in the kitchen as he sliced vegetables on the counter. He turned when he heard me come in, and the second my eyes landed on him, I frowned.

"What?"

I narrowed my eyes in his direction. "You got your hair cut?"

He nodded. "You don't like it?"

It was just a trim, and it looked fine, but that was beside the point. I set down my purse on the table and stalked closer, studying him with an appraising glare. "Who cut it for you?"

He sat down the knife on the chopping block. "My regular girl. I go to a barber shop over on McAllister. Why?"

Now close enough to run my fingers through it, I scoped out the cut. "I like it fine, but I don't understand why you didn't ask me to cut it."

Sullivan placed his hands on my waist and met my eyes. "I didn't even consider you'd want to. I thought I was being helpful by just having it taken care of. I know how busy you are."

I shook my head. "Of course I would want to. Having someone else touch your head is really...intimate." The word out of my mouth surprised us both. I'd never felt this way about a boyfriend in the past, though to be fair, they usually expected free haircuts from the moment we started dating. They didn't care that I booked appointments three months in advance at my salon, they just expected that I'd bring home my scissors and do it in my off-time.

"Especially a woman cutting your hair," I added.

Sullivan raised one eyebrow, and then quickly lowered his mouth to mine for a quick kiss. "Noted. You'll be the only one to cut it from now going forward."

"Okay," I said, still frowning.

Sullivan let out a low chuckle of laughter. "You're adorable when you're jealous. I'll let Will know that his hair is also off-limits."

I planted one hand on my hip. "I'm not jealous,

I'm…"

"You're being territorial. And trust me, it's hot."

I shook my head. "I'm just tired. Don't tease me."

"Fine." He patted me on the butt. "Go take off those shoes. I'm sure they're killing your feet. Then come have a glass of wine. Dinner will be ready in twenty."

Happy to take his suggestion because my feet were killing me, and a glass of wine sounded heavenly, I shuffled into the master bedroom and removed the high-heels, placing them on one of the shelves inside the closet that Will had designated for me. When I returned to the kitchen, a glass of chilled white wine was sitting at the counter in front of a barstool.

I slid myself into it and took a long sip. "Thank you."

"Anything for you, baby." Sullivan flashed me that crooked smile that I loved, and then got back to work chopping and slicing.

A few minutes later, I heard the rattle of keys at the front door. A second later, Will rounded the corner and entered the kitchen.

"Smells good. What's for dinner?" he said to Sullivan

as he joined me by the counter.

"Steak and grilled vegetables," Sullivan replied.

Will placed one hand on my cheek and guided my mouth toward his, stopping just before our lips touched.

He frowned and pulled back.

"What?" I asked.

"Lipstick." He muttered it like it was a curse word.

I'd nearly forgotten. I'd applied red lipstick before work that morning, and had touched it up at the end of the day. Will had given me a hard time—refusing to kiss me before I left and teasing that he was going to institute a no-lipstick rule. I'd only rolled my eyes and laughed, treating Sullivan to a big kiss on his cheek and leaving a red mark on his skin.

"I wouldn't tease her right now, man," Sullivan warned. "I just got a stern talking to about allowing someone else to cut my hair."

I snorted, chuckling into my wineglass.

Will stroked my cheek, his gaze on my mouth again. "You're killing me, sweetheart."

I only rolled my eyes. He could still kiss me if he

really wanted to. It was only lipstick, wasn't like I'd coated my lips with anthrax.

After we'd eaten and the dishes were cleaned up, all three of us retreated to the media room upstairs, Sullivan promising to find the perfect movie we could all agree on. I didn't think it'd be difficult. We generally agreed. Lipstick and haircuts aside. Truthfully, we'd fallen into an easy rhythm as roommates—Sullivan primarily did the cooking and Will and I shared the dishes clean up. It just worked for us.

As Sullivan and Will looked over the new movie releases, I excused myself to the bathroom where I reapplied my lipstick in the mirror, smirking at my reflection.

Feeling bold, I returned to the media room, trying not to smile. I felt almost giddy, like I was taking back power from the ultra-macho Will.

Sullivan's gazed zeroed in on my bold red lips immediately and he shook his head, a mischievous glint in his eyes. I joined them on the couch, sitting down between them, and waited. It only took a second for Will to notice.

And when he did, he let out a groan. "Jesus, babe. More lipstick?"

I smiled and batted my eyelashes. I felt a little evil just then, but he was just so fun to tease. "Kiss me."

Will shook his head slowly. "You're trouble, you know that?"

Turing my head toward Sullivan, he allowed me to press a soft kiss to his lips. He wiped the trace of red away with the back of his hand. But the smile on his lips told me he didn't mind at all.

"Yes, but I'm the best kind of trouble," I murmured.

Sliding from the couch, I lowered myself to my knees on the carpeting in front of Will. With nimble fingertips I began to work at the buckle on his belt.

"What are you ..." the words died on Will's tongue as I unbuttoned his jeans and drew down the zipper.

I was showing him that I had my own opinions, that I held strength in this relationship too, that we were all three on equal footing.

Will's throat moved as he swallowed, his gaze latched on my careful movements as I pushed his boxers down just enough to draw out his cock.

It was already hard but growing firmer by the second. And when I slid my hand along the length of him, he twitched in my palm.

Both men watched as I lowered my face toward Will's lap, placing one kiss against the tip of him. A red lip print stained the head of his cock.

"Oops," I said, blinking up at him.

"Clean it off," Will said, voice impossibly tight.

Leaning forward, I treated him to a long, slow lick, earning me a soft grunt as my tongue swirled around his hot flesh.

I could feel Sullivan's eyes tracking my movements, and it only made me hotter. Knowing he was watching made this feel ten-thousand times more taboo.

"More," Will groaned, leaning back against the couch and lacing his fingers behind his head.

Sullivan slid closer, petting my hair back from my face, and tucking it behind one ear. "You are so fucking sexy," he groaned.

"She's naughty is what she is."

I smiled, my mouth still working, tongue gliding along the firm length of Will's swollen shaft.

"Suck him deeper," Sullivan ordered, his voice a low growl.

The idea that he was getting turned on watching me with Will twisted inside me, sparking a delicious curl of heat low in my belly. And I immediately obeyed, sucking him down as far as I could go, before retreating to draw a shaky breath.

"Faster," Sullivan growled.

I continued treating Will to teasing licks and deep kisses, with both men's breathing growing ragged.

"You're making a mess," Will said, one large palm cupping my cheek.

In the low light of the room, I could see what he meant. His cock held the evidence of my trademark color, the root of him smudged with a distinct ring of red. I was sure it was smeared all to hell across my mouth, too, but I didn't care about that right now. Especially not with the way they were looking at me like I was a goddess reincarnate.

With one hand on the top of my head to guide me,

Will's head fell back against the couch, as I worked up and down over him.

"Gonna come," he murmured. "Get ready for it."

I sealed my mouth around him as hot spurts of cum jetted down my throat and Will let out a low sound of pleasure.

Rising on shaky legs, I excused myself to the bathroom where I cleaned up, and wiped the last traces of lipstick from my mouth. Then I returned to the media room, where Will had fastened his jeans, and he and Sullivan sat in silence, waiting for my return. I almost expected them to pounce on me, but instead, they were watching me with a stunned sort of silence.

I settled down between them and grabbed the remote. "I'm thinking something girly, like a rom-com."

Neither of them said a thing, merely blinking at me as I selected a movie and pressed play.

After several seconds of silence, I patted Will's thigh. "I'm in the mood for some popcorn. Go make me some?"

"Uh." He swallowed. "Yeah. Sure."

When he retreated down the stairs, Sullivan pulled

me into his lap. "I have no idea what's gotten into you, but that was so fucking hot."

Nestled against him, I could feel that he was still hard. I removed myself from his lap and patted his shoulder. "Not right now, tiger, I really do want to watch this movie."

He exhaled slowly and lobbed me a smile. "You really are naughty."

***

Later in bed, Will was sound asleep on my left, and Sullivan was still awake on my right. I'd gotten used to sleeping between them, and now I had no idea how I'd go back to sleeping alone. As far as I was concerned, three definitely was not a crowd. There was something decidedly cozy about it.

"Can't sleep," Sullivan whispered.

"Me neither," I whispered back.

"You horny?" he asked.

I flicked him on the shoulder blade. "You're not getting your dick sucked tonight."

He chuckled. "It was worth a shot."

I rolled my eyes.

"That was really fucking hot," he murmured, trailing his fingertips down my bare spine.

I shrugged. "I really just wanted to teach him a lesson."

I could see Sullivan's answering smile in the near darkness. "I don't think he'll ever hassle you about wearing lipstick again."

Then I'd achieved my goal. As I thought back to tonight in the media room, the memory of Sullivan watching me suck Will off made my heart pump faster.

"Can I ask you something without you freaking out?"

"You can ask me anything," he said.

I chewed on my lower lip, weighing my words. "Have you and Will ever ... done anything sexual together—like just the two of you?"

He didn't answer right away, and in the span of those ten seconds, my heartrate started to climb.

"No," he said finally.

"But tonight, you watched. You're not repulsed by

each other, and sometimes you even seem to appreciate the view."

"Yeah, I guess."

His raw honesty meant everything. I knew that Sullivan would never lie to me. In fact, I knew he'd do everything in his power to make sure I felt safe, happy, and comforted. That did something to a girl. Leaning in closer, I pressed a soft kiss to his lips.

"Have you ever been with a man?" I ventured next.

"A long time ago, yes. But I was young. It was just meaningless experimentation."

"But it wasn't Will?"

"It wasn't Will."

Did that mean that Sullivan was interested in more, but Will wasn't? My mind was spinning with possibilities.

"No more questions. Let's go to sleep."

He patted my butt, silencing the questions that remained unspoken on my tongue

"Goodnight," I said.

Soon, Sullivan's breathing had grown deep and even,

matching Will's. But I knew that sleep was still a long way off for me, as I wondered what this new revelation meant for our future.

Chapter Fifteen

Sullivan

THINGS AT WORK WERE GOING GREAT, and things at home were even better. I'd never met a woman quite like Adrienne before. She was confident and outspoken, but still obedient enough to be everything both Will and I required of her. She couldn't cook to save her life, and she had a bad habit of leaving the toilet seat down, but other than that, I couldn't fault her with a single complaint. And I knew Will felt the exact same way.

It had been three weeks since the repairs in Adrienne's apartment had been completed, and two since she'd decided to sublet the place to a student at the nearby community college. The fact that she'd decided to take the leap of faith and move in with us meant everything.

Except now shit was about to hit the fan. Or, at least that's how it felt. Adrienne's mom was coming to visit this weekend and was set to arrive in the next fifteen minutes. Adrienne had taken off for the airport an hour ago, insistent on collecting her mom alone, and Will and I were tidying the house. It wasn't even messy, yet neither of us could quite seem to sit still. Which was how I found myself sorting through a stack of old junk mail and coupons.

"Do we want this?" I held up a colorful, half-page ad in a flyer to show Will. "Half-priced appetizer at that Irish pub down the road?"

Will shook his head. "You need to relax, dude."

I raised my eyebrows. "And you don't?" I glanced toward where he was frantically wiping down a mirror in the hallway. A mirror that didn't have one single streak.

He blew out a frustrated breath and tossed the paper towel into the trash. "You're right."

I heard the crunch of tires in the driveway and my stomach erupted in nerves. This was it. We knew how incredibly close Adrienne was with her family, and if her mom didn't approve, this could be the end.

"They're here."

I nodded.

We stationed ourselves by the door, both of us milling around nervously. I couldn't recall doing this before—meeting the parents of a girl we were serious about. We'd fielded questions from best friends and over-involved siblings, and even one chick's pastor over the years, but this was new territory for me and Will, and I wasn't exaggerating when I said it fucking terrified me.

I took a deep breath and pulled open the door.

Adrienne's mother was vibrant and attractive with shoulder-length silver hair and bright blue eyes. It was a first-hand look at how Adrienne may look in about thirty years. That thought alone made me smile because she was the face of our future and I loved the way that looked.

"You made it," I called.

Adrienne held her mom's hand, rolling a suitcase with the other. She looked so happy to have her mom here, and her smile was contagious.

Will trotted out to retrieve the suitcase, and followed behind him, stopping in front of Adrienne.

"Sullivan, this is my mom. And Mom, this is Sullivan, and that's Will."

The woman's gaze traveled between us and her lips pursed. Adrienne had explained our relationship over the phone several weeks ago, but seeing it in the flesh was a whole different animal.

She stuck out a hand toward me. "Call me Betsey."

I shook her hand, and then Will did the same. "We're so happy that you're here. Come inside."

When Adrienne had invited her, she'd had to talk her mom into staying here with us, promising that we had plenty of extra bedrooms. Betsey would be staying in the room that I'd vacated ever since Adrienne had moved in and I'd relocated into Will's bedroom to be with them.

Adrienne talked when she was nervous. She gave her mom a tour of the place, Will and I in tow, chatting insistently about every detail from the crown molding to the tankless water heater to the color of the stain on the cabinets. They were details we'd shared with her when she moved in, and I had no idea that she memorized so many of them.

Betsey nodded and smiled at all the right times, but still I wasn't about to let my guard down. I was guessing that Adrienne got her spirit from her mother, which meant we may have to field some tough and honest questions later about our intentions with her daughter.

The tour concluded, a bottle of wine was opened, and still I was waiting for the grilling to start. But it didn't.

Instead Adrienne and her mother sat perched at the kitchen island with their wineglasses as I drew out ingredients for chicken marsala.

As I cooked, Betsey admired my technique, and we shared secrets for grilling fish and how to get roast chicken to come out of the oven perfectly moist. She was pleasant and attentive, and I started to suspect that maybe we'd all made a big deal out of nothing. Perhaps all it was going to take to accept us was to see her daughter happy and in love. And there was no denying that's where this was headed. It was fast, yes, but not unheard of. We'd been living together for a month, and it'd been one of the best months of my life. I knew Will was every bit as smitten with her as I was, which made me bone-deep happy.

During the meal, Betsey indulged in our curiosities about a young Adrienne, painting a picture of a quiet, studious girl who loved her church youth group and cheerleading. Will and I exchanged a look.

After dinner, the dishes were loaded into the dishwasher by Will while I wiped down the table. And then we sat in the living room, Adrienne wedged on the sofa between Will and I, and Betsey sitting in the arm chair across from us, looking down into her third glass of chardonnay.

"So … " she began, her mouth twitching. "About this unique lifestyle of yours…"

"Mom," Adrienne warned, her tone hushed.

I placed one hand on Adrienne's knee, silencing her. "I'm sure you have questions. Fire away."

"We'll be happy to answer any of them," Will added.

Adrienne's eyes pleaded with her mother's, but Betsey ignored her, seemingly emboldened by the glass of wine in her hand. "How long have you two been living this way?"

I looked at Will, pretty sure that he was going to field this particular question.

He nodded, and then his gaze swung over to Betsey. "We met when we were kids staying at the same orphanage, and we quickly became best friends. Over the years, that relationship changed a bit as we grew, our romantic interests aligning, but one thing that never changed and never will is our friendship. We have a mutual respect, and an understanding. We own a home together, a successful business. We've stuck together through it all, and honestly we see no need to part and go our separate ways. I guess you could say we're family. And while we knew that finding a woman to suit us both wouldn't be easy, it's just how we're wired, I guess. Deep down we have pretty traditional values. We want a wife, children someday."

Betsey brought her glass to her lips with trembling fingers. After a long swallow, she exhaled slowly, as though pained. "I'm sorry, I just don't see how something like that could ever work. Not for the long haul anyway. Adrienne's father and I have been married for thirty years, and there's so much compromise, so much open communication needed. Oftentimes it's hard to get two people to see eye to eye, let alone three."

I nodded. "I understand your concern. Truly, I do. I hope that we can prove to you our devotion and maybe even win you over."

Betsey stayed silent, her eyes downcast.

Okay then.

Adrienne gave me a sympathetic look. It wasn't the most promising start, but I wasn't about to give up.

A short time later, Will carried her suitcase upstairs and Adrienne retreated to help Betsey get settled.

By the time she joined us in the bedroom, Will was reading in bed and I'd just finished brushing my teeth.

When Adrienne stepped into the room, it was like all the air had been sucked out. I crossed the room and folded her into my arms. With tears in her eyes, Adrienne pressed her face to my chest. Will rose from the bed and joined us, wrapping Adrienne in his arms as I released her to his grasp. I thought she might cry, but then she drew a deep, shuddering breath and stepped back.

"It's okay," she said.

I couldn't help but smile at her. Here she was the one upset, and still she was consoling us.

I cupped her cheek with my palm. "It will all work out."

Her eyes met mine, and there were huge pools of endless blue.

"You okay, sweetheart?" Will asked.

"I think so," she whispered.

"Let's get you to bed. Come on." I took her hand and led her toward the bed.

Will worked on stripping her out of everything until she stood before us in a pair of light blue cotton panties.

I wanted her. But that was nothing new, I always wanted her. But even more than that, my chest ached for her, and I just wanted to see her smile again.

Reading the mood of the situation apparently faster than me, Will grabbed one of his white t-shirts from the dresser, and helped her pull it on over her head.

"I just want to be held," she said, voice small.

I pulled back the blankets and in we climbed. Will on his side, me on mine, and Adrienne nestled in between us.

"She's allowed to worry. She's your mother," Will said. "But she's wrong, you know? It can work. It will work."

She nodded.

I placed a soft kiss to the back of her neck.

"Get some sleep, baby. Things will look brighter in the morning."

The rest of the weekend passed in a similar fashion. Adrienne stayed tense and nervous, and continued trying to impress her mom. They did various mother/daughter things like shopping, and lunch, and pedicures while Will and I tried to keep ourselves busy. I visited one of the houses we were flipping and worked for several hours, only for something to distract me.

Will and I seemed to share a silent understanding that we weren't going to hide from Betsey who we were or any evidence of our devotion to her daughter. While we were home, we didn't hesitate to hug her, or kiss her goodbye, or show her affection. As far as I was concerned, it was vital. I wanted Betsey to see how much we loved her daughter.

But then Sunday came, and it was time for her to leave for the airport, and I couldn't have been more relieved. I just wanted things to go back to normal. Adrienne climbed into the driver's seat of her car, while Will placed the bags in the trunk, and I touched Betsey's arm, stopping her before she could climb into the car.

"I'm glad you came."

"Thank you for having me," she said. "You have a lovely home."

I smiled at the compliment. "You've raised an amazing daughter, and I hope that you'll give us a chance and accept this, as strange as it might seem to you."

Betsey's gaze softened. "Listen, I think you guys are great, but I'm sorry there is just no way her father will ever go for this, and Adrienne, even though she's a grown woman, she'll always be daddy's girl deep down inside." Her tone was sympathetic, but that didn't ease the blow of her words—not one bit.

Will had closed the trunk and joined us, listening with a pained expression.

"I'm sorry, guys," Betsey finished, and then climbed into the car.

Fuck.

With my heart in my throat, I leaned down to Adrienne's open window and pressed a quick kiss to her lips. "Drive safe, baby."

Will did the same, while Betsey's expression remained stoic as she looked forward through the windshield.

Double fuck.

Chapter Sixteen

Adrienne

I'D JUST finished styling one of my favorite client's hair, when my assistant brought my cell phone over to my station.

"He's called three times. Thought you might want to answer," Amber said.

The caller ID said it was Will. He never called me during the work day. In fact, he hardly ever called me at all. He was more of a texting kind of guy—my man of few words.

"Hello?" I said, answering.

"It's Sull—" Will's voice was breathless and more worried than I'd ever heard it before.

"What's wrong? Did something happen?" My heart rate accelerated as hot fear shot up my spine.

"Yes. We're at Faith Memorial Hospital. Room two-ten. Hurry."

I called out to Tyler that I had to go, grabbed my purse as I all but sprinted to the front door with my heart in my throat.

I'd never been to this hospital before, but the signs were helpful, and I was soon parking in the visitor section and then hustling toward the glass doors of the emergency room.

Not bothering with the elevator, I trotted up the stairs to the second floor and found room two-ten a minute later.

Several things struck me at once. The smell of blood. An empty hospital bed. Will with his hands in his hair, standing in the center of the empty room.

I collapsed into his chest. "What's happening? Is he…"

"I am so sorry. So fucking sorry. I didn't mean to freak you out." Will's expression was pained, but his hands roamed up and down over my arms, soothing me. "There was an accident at one of the houses we're renovating. I freaked out. Fuck. I'm sorry."

"But Sullivan?" my voice broke over his name.

Will nodded. "He's okay. He fell from a scaffolding, broke his arm pretty bad. He may need surgery, but he's okay."

I let out the first deep breath since receiving Will's call thirty minutes ago. My lungs contracted, and Will led me over toward the bed where he lifted me so I sat perched on the edge.

He stepped between my parted knees and held me, patting my back as he spoke. "At first they thought he might have a concussion, but he passed their tests with flying colors. But I heard the words head-injury and I freaked out. I'm sorry for blowing your phone up."

I shook my head. "I'm glad you did. My staff will reschedule the rest of my appointments. This is exactly where I want to be—with you. With Sullivan. Where is he?"

"A specialist is looking at his arm. He'll get a temporary cast tonight and then we can take him home. They'll assess whether he'll need surgery in a few days."

Home.

That word had never sounded better.

I leaned my head against Will's chest again and closed my eyes for a moment. But then noise in the hallway captured my attention.

Being escorted by two women dressed in scrubs, Sullivan was smiling, and had both of them chuckling at something he'd said.

"Baby. You didn't need to miss work for this," he said when he saw me.

I rushed to him, careful not to jostle where his arm rested in a sling, and threw my arms around his neck.

"Of course, I'm here." I didn't mention that Will had been about to lose his shit at the thought of something being wrong with him. I guess I was here as much for Will's emotional needs as I was for Sullivan's injuries. And Will's concern was so sweet and unexpected that it made me feel all soft and melty inside.

Sullivan released me and sat down on the edge of the hospital bed while the doctor turned to face Will and me.

"I'm Dr. Pierson. I'm sorry, but I can't have both of you in here." She turned back to Sullivan. "Is there someone you'd prefer to stay to hear the at-home instructions?"

Sullivan's brow wrinkled. "I'd like both of them to stay. We're in a committed relationship. Asking me to choose between them, Doc, is like asking you to cheat on your husband," he chuckled again.

The doctor's eyebrows shot up. "Both of them?"

Will and I nodded as her eyes swung over to us, appraising, judging.

"We all live together," Sullivan added. "So, yes, any aftercare instructions should be given to both of them."

Dr. Pierson's posture stiffened. "Fine." Her tone was clipped and she looked down at the screen of her tablet, unwilling or maybe just unsure about who to make eye contact with. "Sullivan's suffered a severe break in his forearm that will take time to heal."

Will and I shared a look. The doctor's discomfort was obvious, but I knew neither of us was going anywhere. After she provided us with the aftercare instructions, we took Sullivan home and tucked him into bed.

"What would you like for dinner?" I asked Sullivan where he was propped up on a pillow with the TV on.

"You two are cooking?" He grinned crookedly.

"Of course." I put my hands on my hips. Just because Sullivan was usually the one who cooked dinner didn't mean that Will and I couldn't handle it.

"Surprise me," he said after a moment.

Will and I huddled together in the kitchen and looked through the cabinets. We soon settled on making chicken noodle soup as I started to boil the chicken breasts while he diced vegetables. Once we had put the finishing touches on everything, we carried a tray containing a bowl of steaming soup and a stack of crackers to the bedroom on a tray.

"How are you feeling?" I asked once he'd finished his soup. "Are you sleepy?"

Sullivan shook his head. His eyes were bright and happy. "Horny."

Will chuckled, and I pressed my hand to his cheek. "You can't be serious."

"I'm completely serious."

I shook my head. "You're in no condition to do anything like that. Your arm is in a temporary cast, for heaven's sake."

Sullivan shrugged. "The doctor didn't say anything about abstaining from sexual activity."

Will chuckled. "She would have had a heart attack if we'd asked her about that, as it was she looked like she needed oxygen when we told her we were together."

I took the tray from Sullivan's lap, and after I set it on the dresser, I joined them on the bed and pressed a kiss to his cheek. "There. That will have to do. You need your rest, mister."

Sullivan's gaze darkened and something wicked gleamed in his eyes. "Then I know what I want."

"What's that?" I asked.

"I want to watch you while you fuck Will."

Words failed me. "You what?" I sputtered at last.

I'd never been with just Will before. And certainly not while Sullivan watched. My nipples tinged in my bra at the very idea of it.

"You heard me," Sullivan said, voice low and husky.

Will took my hand and pulled me into his lap. "You heard the man. Come here, sweetheart."

Will kissed my throat and massaged my breasts as I rocked my hips against his growing erection. I looked over at Sullivan, and he was lying back with one arm propped beneath his head, a happy smile on his lips.

"Take out his cock," Sullivan said.

I obeyed, unbuttoning Will's jeans to stroke his firm erection in my hands.

Will grunted, and his eyes slipped closed. "Give him the full show, Adrienne. Strip for me, sweetheart," he said after a few more strokes.

And I did exactly what was in the best interest of the patient.

Chapter Seventeen

Sullivan

IT DIDN'T MATTER that I had a cast on my arm—I knew what I wanted. And I knew I wouldn't be getting to sleep until I had it.

Adrienne rose up on her knees and pushed her leggings and panties down over her hips. Then she was shifting and pulling everything off to toss it on the floor.

I stroked her bare shoulder and she flashed me a smile. She moved back to Will's lap and let out a long exhale as she sank down onto his stiff cock.

I placed my hand on the curve of her bare ass, loving the feel of her flexing and moving over Will.

"So good. So pretty, baby," I murmured, encouraging her. "That's it. Take him deeper."

Adrienne sank all the way down, causing a low groan to rumble in Will's chest.

That was all it took. He gripped her hips roughly in both palms, pulling her down on top of him again and again until they were both panting and breathless.

It was so incredibly erotic to watch, better than any porn because I knew these 'characters' intimately and they were not only performing for my benefit, but for their own release, as well. My heart thumped hard and fast and my skin felt flushed. "Squeeze him, baby. Squeeze your pussy around his cock," I said, still gripping one of her fleshy ass cheeks as she moved up and down.

I knew the moment she obeyed my command because Will's eyes sank closed and he moaned.

Moments later, with an appreciative glance toward me, Adrienne came apart in his arms, and Will wasn't far behind, his breaths coming fast as he came hard, as he finished inside her.

Adrienne climbed off Will's lap and over toward me. She placed a tender kiss on my lips.

"You're a naughty patient."

I merely smirked, not disagreeing.

Her hand went to my lap and dipped beneath the waistband of my sweatpants. "Hmm. What's this?" she whispered.

I groaned when she slid her palm over my erection,

then reached for her breasts and pinched one taut nipple. She groaned and sensation shot through my body.

Adrienne fisted my cock and jacked me slowly until I came all over her hand. After that, I was so drowsy and spent, I barely stayed awake long enough to watch them clean me up and fuss over me. It was then that I decided maybe having a broken arm wouldn't be the worst thing in the world.

Chapter Eighteen

Adrienne

"Better?" I asked. I couldn't keep a mischievous grin from spreading across my face as I watched Will bring his morning cup of coffee to his lips.

He took a healthy sip of the steaming brew, his eyes locking with mine as he swallowed.

"Worse," he grunted, setting the mug down on the counter.

"What'd you buy this time, butterscotch or hazelnut?" Sullivan asked, turning to flash me a smile from the stove where he had happily returned to making his own scrambled eggs.

I giggled, a familiar, heady feeling washing over me. I loved toying with Will, reminding him that I could be equally as strong and as opinionated about things, too. And it drove me the best kind of crazy when Sull played along.

"Guess again," I teased, raising an eyebrow in Will's direction.

"No way I'm taking another sip." He crossed his arms, leaning his hips back against the counter.

A power move? That's not the game we're playing today.

"I'd be careful if I were you. I have all kinds of methods of persuasion." I leaned forward in my seat and rested on my elbows, a smirk on my face that basically told him not to tempt me. The neckline on my pale pink blouse was just low enough that I knew Will had a peek at what was hidden beneath.

"I'm familiar," Will said, a small smile escaping from the corner of his lips.

"Just drink the damn coffee, we've got a demo day to start." Sullivan scooped his eggs onto a plate and carried it over to the breakfast table.

It had been six weeks since Sullivan's injury, and things were finally starting to feel normal again around the house. Not that a broken arm had affected his sex drive at all. If anything, we had all gotten more creative than ever. Something about switching between being a doting nurse by day and a sexy goddess at night was thrilling to me. If I wasn't sure I'd be into ménage at first, these past few weeks made it clear. I couldn't imagine going back to just being with one man at a time, but more than that, I couldn't imagine my life without Will and Sullivan in it. Though it was nice that his cast was finally removed.

"Ready," Will grunted, gulping down the last of his coffee.

"Final answers?" I arched an eyebrow while Will squinted into his cup.

"Dog shit." He was testing me now.

Sullivan laughed. "Based on the smell, I'll put my money on…cinnamon roll?"

"You're both wrong." I slid down from my chair to stand between them. "Amaretto."

"Sounds like French for dog shit."

I gave Will a playful glare before turning to grab the stainless steel to-go mug I'd prepared for him earlier. "Here."

"What's this?" He cocked an eyebrow in my direction.

"Regular, black, boring coffee. Just for you."

Will smiled and pressed a kiss to the top of my head.

I turned toward Sullivan, placing my hands on his chest. "Remind me again about the new safety procedures you put in place at work?"

"I'll do you one better. I wrote them down so you didn't think of something during the day and start to worry." Sullivan pulled a folded-up sheet of paper out of the back pocket of his jeans and held it in front of his chest.

His thoughtfulness touched me. "I appreciate that." I reached for the paper, but before I could grab it, he pulled it out of my reach.

"Gotta plant one on me before I fork it over. Doctor's orders."

I rolled my eyes. "I don't remember Dr. Pierson saying anything about prescribing kisses. And trust me, I was paying close attention."

"I don't know, I'm pretty sure she added the kisses at the end. You must have been in the bathroom or something. Right, Will?"

"Couldn't hurt."

I crossed my arms. Part of me wanted to feel annoyed when they ganged up on me like this. But the other part of me? Was really freaking into it. Especially because I knew it was all in good fun.

Lifting up on my toes, I pressed my lips against Sullivan's, feeling Will's gaze on us as we kissed.

"Thank you, babe," Sullivan said sweetly, handing me the paper.

I quickly unfolded it, scanning the page to see if there were any possible dangerous scenarios they'd overlooked. I knew I was being paranoid, but I still hadn't forgotten how terrifying it was when I thought something horrible had happened to him. And the thought of something like that happening again—or worse? To either of them? That was enough to make a girl downright clinical.

"Anything we missed?" Will asked, placing his hands on my hips and reading the list over my shoulder.

"Nothing I can think of, at least. You two should probably go. I don't want to make you late for demo day."

"She's right," Sullivan said, checking the clock over the stove. "We should probably get going."

Will placed a quick peck on one cheek, and Sullivan swooped in to kiss the other. The whole twice the affection thing? I had really come to love it.

"Do you want me to pick anything up from the store on my way home from work?" I asked as the two of them made their way to the garage.

"I think we're all set. Just bring your pretty little ass back to us in one piece," Sullivan replied.

"We've got something planned," Will added, all matter-of-fact.

"A surprise?" My eyes widened.

"You'll see." Will turned and flashed one of his rare, sweet grins at me before closing the door behind them both.

What the two of them were planning was beyond me. But by that point, I was pretty sure that whatever it was, I would absolutely love it.

***

With the promise of a special surprise in mind, the rest of my day went by in a snap, and before I knew it, I was sweeping up the hair of my last client and closing up shop for the day.

When I walked through the door, I was greeted by

the heavenly smell of toasted almonds and the heavenly sight of my two favorite guys preparing dinner in the kitchen. Well, one of my favorite guys was preparing dinner. Will was sitting at the counter, sipping water and chatting while Sullivan sautéed something green and healthy-looking.

Will poured me a glass of wine, and dinner was ready within ten minutes. We chatted casually throughout dinner, they filled me in on demo day and I shared some stories of Tyler's latest antics, and as easy as the conversation was, I was still dying to know what those two had up their sleeves.

"So," Sullivan began, swirling the berry-colored liquid in his wineglass, "Will and I have placed a bet."

"Oh?" I could feel an excited blush creeping over my neck.

"We want to see how many times we can make you come," Will said bluntly.

I was sure the blush had taken over my face by that point. My heart pounded in my chest.

"Do you?"

They both nodded.

Oh my.

Without another word, Sullivan rose to his feet, and offered me his hand. The dinner dishes could wait. Will framed my other side as they guided me into the bedroom and up on the bed.

Things started slow, with lots of kisses, and grinding, until I was soaking wet, and so ready to be naked. Will pulled my shirt off from over my head and unsnapped my bra a second later. It joined my shirt on the floor. And then his hot mouth was on my nipples, and Sullivan was unbuttoning my jeans.

With my heartbeat pounding out a fast rhythm inside my ribcage, I watched in awe as Sullivan's mouth moved to my pussy, treating me to slow, teasing licks, as Will continued sucking my firm nipples into his mouth. Way too soon, I was grabbing onto Sullivan's hair and coming apart under the swirling of his skilled tongue.

He raised his head from between my legs and gave me a crooked grin. "That's one."

"My turn," Will said, trading places with Sullivan so that he could bring his mouth to my core. Without giving me time to gather myself, or prepare, his wicked lips were moving against me, as sensation pooled low at the base of my spine all over again.

Much sooner than I thought possible, my back arched and I gave a shout. "Will!"

One thick finger pushed into me as Sullivan bit down lightly on my breasts.

I came apart again.

"Two," Will murmured, voice husky.

The next half hour passed this way until we passed number five, and I was breathless, boneless, and completely exhausted in a way I'd never experienced before.

Lying back against the pillows, I peeked open one eye. Sullivan and Will were kneeling over me, both now stripped down to their birthday suits.

"She's exhausted," Sullivan said.

"We wore her out, I guess," Will added.

I tried reaching for them, but my arms felt limp and useless, dropping to the bed beside me. "It's okay, I can ..." I yawned and forgot what I was going to say mid-sentence.

"She can't handle us both right now."

"Flip a coin?"

"Sounds good…but I'm not sure if I want 'heads' or 'tails' as my choice. What say you, Will?"

"For sure, head—I mean, heads—for me." And then they both looked down upon me like I was their queen and let the flip of a coin decide who got to pleasure me next.

Chapter Nineteen

Adrienne

"VEGAS, BABY!" TYLER AND I squealed, clinking our apple martinis together and shimmying on our stools.

"To becoming better color mixologists," I giggled, raising my glass in the air.

Tyler rolled his eyes. "If I have to hear one more bad hair pun, I'm going to stab someone with her own sheering scissors."

"Oh, come on, you love it."

"Girl, I love you, but if you keep this up, I'm ditching class tomorrow and taking myself to Cirque du Soleil."

Every year, the two of us flew to a different part of the country to attend a hair stylist training conference. We both loved what we did, and it was important to us to stay up to date on the latest trends and techniques. This year, we found a two-day training class in Las Vegas that looked perfect. And a little intense. We spent the entire day bouncing from lecture to demonstration to practice, but it was worth it. And we'd definitely earned ourselves a few drinks at the hotel bar.

"Ugh, my feet are killing me," Tyler sighed, examining a blister on the back of his heel.

"I told you comfortable shoes would be a must," I said, eyeing his lime green, pointed-toe, patent leather flats.

"You only get one shot at a first impression." He shrugged, lifting his leg into the air. "Better make it fabulous."

I laughed and rolled my eyes. "And the pink highlights aren't enough of an impression?"

"With a bunch of stylists? Girl, please. And look who's talking, little miss fire engine red stilettos."

"Hey, I'm not the one complaining about foot pain."

"No, you're the one who's stalling." Tyler crossed his legs and arched an eyebrow. "We've been gone for twenty-four hours, and you haven't spilled a single detail about your crazy, three-way sex life."

A blush crept over my chest as my thoughts travelled to the other night.

"I mean, what can I say? It's incredible. Will and

Sullivan are incredible. Best sex I've ever had, hands down. And the best boyfriends, if I'm being honest."

Tyler narrowed his eyes. "Two hunky, macho men who are great in bed? Shocking. Details, Adrienne, I need details."

"Well, for starters, fucking is like an Olympic sport for them." I guess the liquor has loosened my tongue more than I thought. But my heart rate quickened just at the thought of what they could do. How they took turns pleasuring me until I was limp, useless putty in their arms. The two of them carrying me to the bed and then later to the shower was becoming a part of our routine.

"Are we talking bronze medalist Olympics, or…?"

"Oh, gold medalist, for sure. Both of them. They know what they're doing."

"Two gold medalists? Lucky dicks … I mean, ducks." Tyler downed his martini and shook his head. "And I thought I was doing well for myself."

"Honestly, the best part is how attentive they are. They're both so thoughtful and loving…they make me feel completely worshipped."

Tyler's eyebrows shot up. "Well, shit. Sounds like they've got the whole feelings thing down, too."

I nodded, my heart swelling in my chest. It was dawning on me that I'd be sleeping alone for the first time in a long time that night. And the thought of getting under the covers without Will and Sullivan's hard, strong bodies on either side of me? Without their tender kisses and cuddles to wake me up? Let's just say I wasn't looking forward to it.

"Here's the real question," Tyler said, cutting off my sad thoughts, "which one has a better dick? I'm not talking about size, we both know that's subjective. I mean, which one feels more like…the right fit?"

I laughed and shook my head. "Not a chance."

"Girl, now is hardly the time to play coy. It's just you and me. And you know I can keep a secret." He rested his elbows on the bar top, nodding slowly and giving me a mischievous grin.

I rolled my eyes.

"They're both perfect."

Tyler wiggled his eyebrows.

"And they both fulfill me in *different* ways, together they make this relationship the perfect combination of everything a woman could want," I added with a wink.

Tyler gasped, his eyes wide with excitement. "Ooh, we've got some variety going on here, I see. Even better, how fun for you. And I'm totally not the slightest bit jealous." His sly grin said otherwise.

I smiled and shook my head. That's about as much as I was willing to reveal about Will and Sullivan's intimate details. I'm all for girl talk, but Tyler will probably meet them one day. And the thought of him looking at them with X-ray vision? Not exactly my idea of a good time.

I pulled out my phone and checked the time—9:15. I knew it was two hours later for Will and Sullivan, but the thought of falling asleep without even talking to them made my heart sink. I swallowed the last of my apple-tini and hopped down from the barstool.

"Be right back," I told Tyler, then I made my way to an empty and quieter section of the lobby to call them.

After a few rings, Sullivan's voice greeted me. "Hey, babe. How's Vegas?"

I couldn't help a huge grin spreading across my face

at the sound of his voice. "Hi, Sull, Vegas is good. But it'd be even better if you and Will were here with me."

"Yeah? Good, I'm glad you're enjoying it."

Something in his voice didn't sit well with me, but I brushed it off. He probably just had a long day at work. The new house they were renovating had been keeping them so busy with repairs that hadn't been expected.

"How are you? How's Will? What are you two up to?"

"We're good, you know, just hanging out at home. Business as usual."

"What did you end up making for dinner? Ours was catered, but I swear your food is better."

"Just grilled some steak and veggies." His voice sounded flat. Strained.

Worry began to gnaw at my insides. I was about to ask Sullivan what was going on when I heard it. Heard *her*. A woman's voice in the background, talking to what sounded like Will. A voice I didn't recognize. A voice I knew nothing about.

The air rushed out of my lungs, and it felt like a lead

weight was dropped in my stomach.

What the fuck is going on?

I'd only been gone one day, and while I would have sworn I knew them inside and out, believed everything I'd just told Tyler, now I was starting to realize, maybe I didn't really know them at all.

All I could muster to say to him was, "Tyler just came out of the bathroom, I better let you guys go. Talk to you later."

And I hung up the phone feeling that there was more than hundreds of miles separating the three of us than I'd have ever imagined.

Chapter Twenty

Sullivan

SETTING THE VASE in the center of the table, I dropped in the flowers and gave them a good once-over. I'd taken my time picking them out at the florist, and I wanted to make sure they looked perfect. Sighing, I took a few steps back to take in the view before me. With the lilies and the "welcome home" banner, the space looked a little more festive. I'd already assembled a cheese board, and the second Adrienne walked through the door, we'd pop open a bottle of champagne. Just as I was about to check the time, Will walked in and whistled.

"Looks great," he said, eyeing the flowers. "Lilies?"

I shrugged. "They reminded me the most of her." They were elegant and striking, and strong yet delicate at the same time.

He nodded and took a seat at the counter. "When should she get here?"

"Any minute now."

Like clockwork, the moment the words left my

mouth, I heard a car door closing in front of the house. Adrienne's coworker Tyler had parked his lime green roller skate of a car at the airport, and had insisted he'd drop her off on his way home.

Will and I rose to greet her at the door, smiling broadly as it swung open. Even in yoga pants and a soft cotton t-shirt, Adrienne looked gorgeous. She'd only been gone a couple days, but the subtle stirring behind my zipper was enough of a reminder that I didn't want her to ever leave again.

"Welcome home," I said, leaning in for a kiss. But before I could make contact, Adrienne turned her cheek, so my lips never met their intended target. I frowned. What the fuck? Not quite the hello I was expecting.

"Let me take that," Will said, grabbing her small suitcase and taking it to the bedroom hallway. He was better at hiding it, but I knew he was every bit as confused as I was.

Adrienne didn't say a word as she brushed past me into the kitchen, where she stood by the counter with her arms folded. She didn't seem to notice the flowers or the banner. Or rather, if she did, she was choosing to ignore them.

Will joined us in the kitchen, frowning at the tension between us. He gave me a quick look, and I returned it with a subtle shake of the head. Neither of us knew what was going on.

"Can I get you anything? I made us a cheese board, and we have some champagne." I pulled the bottle out of the fridge, ready to pop it open.

"I heard a woman here last night," Adrienne said, her eyes shooting daggers as they bore into mine.

Shit.

I set the unopened bottle on the counter, and Will and I exchanged a look.

"Let's sit," Will said, motioning her over to the table.

With her arms still crossed, Adrienne sat in the far chair, the look on her face angrier than I'd ever seen her. It was obvious, I'd fucked up last night by not telling her Layla was here when she called. Honestly, I just didn't want to freak her out.

"The woman you heard last night," I began, folding my hands on the table, "was our ex. But it's not what you think. Nothing happened. She just showed up out of nowhere, asking for another chance."

Adrienne's face fell. Somehow the hurt look was even worse than the angry one. "And?"

"We said no," Will said, his eyes locked on hers.

Adrienne sighed, a look of confusion washing over her face. She turned to stare out the window, still processing what she'd just heard.

I had no idea she'd overheard Layla last night. Truthfully, she wasn't here very long, and we'd sent her away. And while Will and I had no plans to hide the truth, I just figured we'd explain the scenario in person—after we made up for the lost time together.

"She showed up here, she'd been drinking and had taken a ride here, and gotten dropped off. We let her in while we called a cab. And we only talked for a few minutes, but I think it helped her to get the closure she needed," I said.

Just when I thought we were in the clear, her eyes snapped back over to our faces—and she still looked pissed.

"Listen," she said, pushing her long, honey-colored hair out of her face, "if we're going to be in this relationship we need to set some ground rules."

Will and I nodded, smart enough to know that it was our turn to listen.

"If you had no interest in getting back together with her, why did you even let her in in the first place? And why were you so weird about it on the phone? You could have just told me what was going on instead of making it a secret the two of you were trying to keep from me since you didn't want to tell me over the phone."

"I'm sorry, you're right," I said, a pit forming in my stomach. It killed me to think that she didn't trust us. But I also knew we'd fucked up. She had every right to be mad, and we only had ourselves to blame.

"No more secrets," she continued. "The only way this is going to work is if we are all open and honest. It's hard enough to trust one person in a relationship. But if it feels like two are ganging up on the other? Forget it. That'll never work."

Echoes from her mom's visit were reverberating around in my head at what she said and I wondered if Will and Adrienne were thinking the same thing.

When she was finished, the three of us sat there in silence. Suddenly the decorations for the party seemed ridiculous. Part of me wanted to rip the welcome home banner off the wall and shove it in the trash.

Adrienne stood up. "All I want to do right now is take a hot shower and go to bed."

As she left the room, Will and I watched in somber silence. He might not have been the most expressive guys around, but I always knew when Will was upset. And between the two of us, the energy in the room was at an all-time low.

We exchanged a look, and the air between us changed.

"Fuck this," Will grunted.

I nodded, and we both rose to follow her. We were going to fight for our girl.

Wordlessly, Will and I both knew what we had to do. We had to go after her. Show her how *very* sorry we were, how much we adored her. She had every right to be angry, but I couldn't stand feeling that way for the rest of the night. We were going to make it up to her, one way or another.

We entered the master bath, where steam was already fogging up the mirror. Will and I removed our clothes as we approached the shower door, admiring Adrienne's perfect silhouette through the glass. We stepped into the shower, waiting on the other side of the water for her to allow us to join.

"Do you have room for two more?"

Adrienne turned, her wet hair cascading down over her shoulders, the intoxicating smell of her shampoo filling the air. Squaring her shoulders at us, she narrowed her eyes.

"Have you two idiots learned your lesson?" Her voice was sharper, more demanding than I was expecting.

"Yes," Will said, voice firm.

"So much, yes. We promise," I added.

Her eyes moved lazily over our bodies before she nodded, and the two of us moved to stand on either side of her. Soon, she was sandwiched between us, stroking us both along our chests and shoulders. It felt amazing to have the three of us together again, and it took every ounce of self-restraint to keep myself from grabbing her ass. Something told me we weren't quite in the clear—not just yet.

"I've thought of a way you both can make it up to me," Adrienne said, patting our chests.

Will and I stood in silence, awaiting her command.

"I want you two to kiss."

Chapter Twenty-one

Adrienne

MY HEART WAS POUNDING as I looked from Sullivan's face to Will's, waiting for their answer.

I'd challenged them to kiss. Something I'd been curious about for a while. Ever since Sullivan watched me pleasure Will that night, and then his late-night confession that he'd messed around with a guy in the past, my interest was piqued about what their boundaries were.

And now this was it. The moment where I'd find out the extent of their feelings for each other. Over the course of the past several weeks, I'd begun to sense their attraction to each other, in addition to me, but part of me had just dismissed it, thinking I was probably crazy.

But seeing as they were both desperate to please me, now seemed like the best time to bring it up.

Tension hung in the air between us, swirling like steam from the hot water.

Neither of them budged. Were they stunned by my request?

Sullivan's gaze, bright and inquisitive, slid up to Will's, whose face was so expressionless, it was impossible to read. But going by Will's posture—his ramrod straight spine, his shoulders square, something about my request made him uncomfortable.

I blew out a slow sigh, letting my hands drop to my sides. "Never mind. Maybe I'm not in the mood for a shower after all."

"Wait."

Before I could move, Sullivan's voice stopped me. He scanned my face and then looked to Will, gently touching his fingers to his shoulder.

"You okay with this?"

Will's eyes flitted from mine to the floor before briefly meeting Sullivan's. He made some wordless sound of acceptance, unable to put into words what he was thinking. But he wasn't backing down. My heart thumped quickly in my chest.

Keeping his hand on Will's shoulder, Sullivan stepped toward him. Watching their two naked bodies, wet with hot water, standing just inches apart, almost caused my brain to short circuit. Their cocks hung heavily between them, soft, but still impressive. So close to touching ….

Their lips met, pressing together with a tenderness I wasn't expecting. Sullivan tilted his head, his eyelashes fluttering. It only lasted a few seconds, but it was by far the hottest thing I'd ever seen.

Sullivan stepped back, and Will kept his eyes trained to the tile at our feet.

"Happy now?"

I smiled, placing my hands on both of their chests. "Very. In fact, I think you two deserve a reward."

Running one hand up each of their chests, I loved the way their muscles stiffened under my touch. Together, they stood motionless, letting me explore for several long minutes. While I caressed muscles, and leisurely stroked them, Sullivan pressed tender kisses between my shoulder blades, and Will touched my face, my breasts, silently watching as I explored.

"Should we take this into the bedroom?" Will asked, nuzzling his mouth against my neck.

I shook my head. After the long flight I'd had, I felt like freshening up. "I did actually want to shower."

Sullivan positioned me under the spray of the water and massaged floral-scented body wash over my skin.

Once I was thoroughly washed and the soapy bubbles were rinsed from my skin, Will's mouth kissed a path down my neck, to my breasts where he suckled each pebbled nipple into his mouth as Sullivan's hand slid between my legs.

Soon I was a writhing, moaning mess of desire under their skilled touches. Then my back was pressed against Will's broad chest, and Sullivan took his turn kissing my lips and plucking my aching nipples with skilled touches.

"I want you. Both of you," I murmured, reaching one hand into Will's hair as he stood behind me, rubbing my hips against Sullivan's pelvis.

I felt a warm current of unspoken communication run between the men in the span of about three seconds, and then Will was running his hands over the flesh of my ass and leaning down to whisper near my ear.

"Can I fuck you here, sweetheart?"

My eyes flew open and found Sullivan's blue gaze. The hungry, half-lidded expression in his eyes almost undid me. Yet, it was the idea of finally having them both at once that sent me careening toward bliss.

"Y-yes … show me," I murmured, leaning back to meet Will's gaze.

His mouth captured mine in a hot kiss, and his answering groan told me everything I needed to know. H'd b̲ ̲ ̲ ̲ ̲ ̲ ̲ patiently for this moment.

want to do this here?" Sullivan asked, as he guided me to his mouth for a

or us both. "I can prepare her here."

grabbed the bottle of coconut oil he topic was settled.

for some pain, I was prepared for very least a bit of awkwardness, but ely not prepared for was the slow, teasing sensuality and the blinding pleasure that came with Will's naughty caresses.

While Sullivan dropped to his knees and feasted on the wet, slippery flesh between my legs, Will's fingers did the most amazing things to my backside that I hadn't expected to like quite so much.

"You're so sexy, sweetheart," Will murmured sweet compliments in my ear, biting my neck as his clever fingers made deft work of preparing me. But the words to respond were nowhere to be found because Sullivan's tongue sent me straight into a body-quaking release faster than either of them could say ménage.

Sullivan rose to his feet, and his cocky smirk made me laugh, despite the overwhelming intensity of the moment.

"Put your hands on my shoulders, baby," he said, as he lifted my thigh, securing it around his hip.

Will grabbed more coconut oil, and generously applied it to himself and me.

Gripping Sullivan's shoulders, I felt the energy in the steamy shower change. This was it. This was what it was like to have two boyfriends, and the question of if I could handle it hung in the air between us.

"You'll tell me if we give you more than you can handle?" Sullivan's voice was incredibly tight, and I watched with hooded eyes as he gripped his length in his fist and gave a leisurely stroke.

"I promise," I murmured, arching my back toward

Will who was erotically rubbing his firm dick between my ass cheeks and trailing wet kisses at the back of my neck.

I never thought I'd be this hot—this bothered—this ready, but I felt like if they didn't take me right this instant, I was going to burst.

"Will, Sul … I need you to take me now." And with that, the challenge was accepted.

While Sullivan supported my weight, and pushed his length into my hot channel, Will waited patiently until Sullivan was fully buried within me, and we let out a collective groan. Then ever so slowly, Will began to thrust behind me, working himself into my snug back opening with patience and skill.

I couldn't think, I couldn't speak. All I could do was feel. Feel the love and attention that they both were raining down upon me and it was overwhelming in such a fantastic way.

"That's it," Will encouraged, his voice a harsh growl. "Fuck."

Desire and heat swamped all my other senses. The only thing that existed in this moment was us. Our pleasure.

"So. Fucking. Good." Sullivan let out a sexy moan as he bit down on my collarbone, his thrusts slow and deep.

"Breathe for me, sweetheart," Will encouraged.

I inhaled sharply as I felt him slip inside farther, my fingernails biting into Sullivan's shoulders.

"Push your ass back, baby," Sullivan murmured, slowing his pace. "Take his cock."

Their dirty endearments always succeeded into turning me into a melty puddle of hormones, but I did as Sullivan's steady voice instructed, experimentally giving my hips a little push back.

"Just like that," Sullivan groaned.

Will bit out another curse word and I felt a full-body moan shudder through him. "You look so sexy with my cock buried in your tight ass."

The dueling sensations were overwhelming in the best possible way. I'd never heard Will make the sexy, breathy noises he was currently making against the back of my neck. Or seen the look of admiration and wonder that was currently reflected in Sullivan's gaze. I wished I could see both of their faces while we were all joined in a trifecta of bliss and eroticism.

When I looked up at Sullivan, I noticed he was watching Will with a look of desire written all over his features. It seemed like more than appreciation of this moment, it seemed, like, well I wasn't sure. But it made something inside my belly twist in confusion. But before I could ponder it further, Will thrust harder, stealing my breath as he buried himself completely.

My body was limp between them as they pushed and pulled and thrusted, and soon I was shuddering through a release so powerful, I thought I might pass out. Sullivan's firm grip around me was the only thing keeping me from collapsing onto the shower floor.

And then he was joining me in bliss, tipping over the edge as his cock jerked inside me. By the time Will's sexy grunts increased in frequency, I could hardly stand. He came hard, pulling out to paint my backside in his hot semen.

Things from there passed in a blur. I was kissed and caressed and washed from head to toe all over again, including my hair which they lovingly shampooed and conditioned before wrapping me in fluffy towels and carrying me over to the bed, where I struggled to keep my eyes open as they climbed in beside me, cocooning me in warmth.

"I love you," I whispered into the darkness. "Both of you."

My heart was in my throat as the seconds ticked past. *Had they heard me?*

"Been waiting for you to get here. I love you, too, baby." Sullivan pressed a kiss to my forehead.

Will's hand found mine under the blanket. "Love you, sweetheart. You're ours now."

"Yes. Yours ... and yours." I yawned. I heard them chuckle.

My smile refused to fade even as I drifted off into a deep sleep.

***

"One carton of fresh blueberries, just like you asked for," Sullivan said, setting a paper bag on the counter.

I'd woken up to a growling stomach—and a craving

for blueberry muffins fresh out of the oven. Given how amazing last night was, it made complete sense that I was starving this morning.

Sullivan had gone to the store to pick up the blueberries while I began making the batter. Cooking might not have been my forte, but when it came to baking? My mom had taught me right. There was something so gratifying about it, too—the calm preciseness of measuring and mixing, the waiting while the house filled with the glorious scents of vanilla and cinnamon.

"Thank you, Sull." I gave him a quick kiss before grabbing the bag he'd left for me on the counter.

"Not too sore, are you?" he asked, lips lingering on my neck.

I shook my head, visions of last night's naughty shower escapades dancing through my head.

Then he joined Will at the table. The two of them were drinking coffee and talking about their latest project.

"You thinking granite for the countertops, or something else?" Will asked him.

Sullivan shook his head. "I want to try that new

quartz product that came out recently. It could be really pretty with a subway tile backsplash."

I folded the blueberries into the batter, my mind wandering to the shower last night.

I had fallen ass over stilettos for these two big, sexy men, something I swore I'd never do. And our relationship was so much more than just hot sex, so much more than what I ever thought a *threesome* could be. Sullivan was sweet, and thoughtful, and made me laugh easier than anyone ever had before—he had this way about him that made all my stress vanish the moment he walked into a room and lopped one of those sexy smirks my way. He lit me up like sunshine on a cloudy day, he was so real and so honest and also really fucking sexy.

Will was his polar opposite in many ways. Moody, demanding, and intense. Sexy in a different way—raw, carnal and completely masculine. He was a tortured soul, a former orphan with a steely exterior wall built up, but sweet with me at the same time. Winning him over, watching him let me in—there was nothing quite like it.

Practically on cue, Will looked over at me. "How's the batter?"

"You can try it if you'd like."

The two of them joined me at the counter, each running a finger up the side of the bowl. Once the batter hit his tongue, Sullivan groaned.

"That's incredible, babe."

Will grunted in agreement. They both kissed me on the cheek before I shooed them away. I needed to start spooning the batter into the muffin pan. They smiled at each other and shook their heads before sitting back down at the table.

One of them would have been enough, but the two of them together were the ultimate package. No matter what kind of mood I was in—I had the perfect companion. And I knew they would have each taken a bullet for me. I felt so safe and protected and cherished.

But as good as things had been, lately something had begun to nag at me. A feeling I'd get in the pit of my stomach when the three of us were together. A glance that lasted too long between them, an inside joke I wasn't privy to, the way they seemed to communicate through unspoken glances over my head.

But it was more than just that. I'd started to notice

things in the bedroom felt different, too. The way Sullivan watched Will's powerful hips thrust into me with a look of sheer lust on his face. The way Will's expression turned pained when Sullivan would take himself in hand and stroke while Will made love to me. All the while Will refused to make eye contact with Sullivan.

But there was no denying their chemistry after last night's kiss.

The connection they had was so special, so different from what they had with me. It wasn't that I was jealous—not one bit—they made me feel like a goddess practically every night. I just couldn't help but pick up on the small ways I was outside what they had, what they'd shared before I came along. And I wasn't sure they were aware of how rare what they had really was.

"You okay?" Will was suddenly by my side, staring at me with worried, furrowed brows.

I'd completely zoned out. I didn't even hear the oven ding that it was done preheating. I forced a smile and nodded my head.

"I'm fine, just a little tired from last night, I think." I met Will's eyes, which were still dark and concerned. He nodded but didn't look convinced.

"Are you sure? You've seemed a little tense all morning." Sullivan joined us by the counter, running his large, strong hand down my spine.

I shook my head again. "Really, I'm okay. Just tired. And ready for some muffins," I said as cheerily as I could, shrugging Sullivan's hand off my shoulders. I slid the muffin tin into the oven, making sure to set the timer— the one step I was known for forgetting.

Will and Sullivan exchanged another look. They knew me better than I realized sometimes. And that made it hard to hide anything from them.

But I couldn't bring myself to tell them the truth. Not yet. What we had was so close to perfect. The last thing I wanted to do was go and ruin it.

Chapter Twenty-two

Adrienne

MOVING MY SCISSORS quickly through the split-ends of my client's hair, I let the pieces fall to the floor.

"You know, sweetie, you really should be using a heat protectant every time you straighten. Your beautiful curls just can't handle two piping ceramic plates squeezing the life out of them day after day without a little added protection," I said, giving the redheaded teenage girl in my chair my nicest, most helpful smile.

She nodded and smiled weakly before turning back to her phone, her thumbs moving rapidly over the screen.

"How often do you straighten it?" I held her damaged ends between my fingers. Judging by their straw-like texture, I'd have put my money on just about every day.

"Uh, I don't know. For, like, school days? And sometimes on the weekend."

"Hmmm…well, it looks like you have a really beautiful, natural texture. Is it okay if once I finish up this cut, I use one of our curl enhancers to show you an easy way to style it?"

The girl's eyes snapped up to meet mine in the mirror. They were wide and hesitant, and her eyebrows were raised, but she didn't look like she was totally against it.

"If you hate it, I'll straighten it for you. With heat protectant, of course." I didn't think it'd come to that, but I was used to teenage anxiety when it came to hair.

"Okay...sure, why not?" She shrugged, trying to hide the small smile creeping over her face. I'd decided from the moment she sat down in my chair that I'd win this girl over. And based on that small victory, I think I was on the right track.

Carefully trimming her ends while not taking off too much length, I finished up the cut and moved on to styling. Just like I thought, my favorite curl enhancer worked wonders on this girl's neglected tresses, and by the time I finished the blowout with the diffuser, she looked like a whole new woman.

I spun her around in the chair, finally revealing the new life of her curls.

"What do you think?"

"Oh my God, I love it! You're the best!"

I smiled and shook my head, topping her look off with some hair spray before sending her off with a bottle of the curl enhancer for herself.

Once my client left, Tyler plopped down in my chair.

"Mexican or Mediterranean?" he asked, wiggling his eyebrows in excitement.

"Mexican, duh. Who do you think I am?"

The two of us quickly closed the salon for lunch, walking to our favorite Mexican place around the corner.

We both got our usual orders, which was chicken tacos for me, and a burrito bowl for Tyler, with an order of chips and guacamole for us to share.

We ate in silence for a couple minutes before Tyler gave me a quizzical look.

"What's up with you today, girl? You're quieter than usual."

"Me? What do you mean? Did you see how chatty and helpful I was with Sharon's daughter?" The redhead was related to one of our highest-paying clients, and our appointment today was one of the first I had with her that didn't include at least three eye-rolls.

"Mhmm." Tyler arched an eyebrow, taking a long sip of his iced tea. "Something's up. Spill."

I sighed. Tyler was right, of course. The strange feeling I'd had the other day hadn't gone away…in fact, it had gotten worse. And as hesitant as I was to admit it to anyone, even myself, I knew that Tyler would be my most empathetic audience.

I wiped my hands on my napkin and let out a sigh. "It's the guys. Don't get me wrong, things are great. Will and Sullivan are still as sweet and loving as ever, the sex is amazing, I'm never bored…"

"But?" One well-sculpted eyebrow darted up.

"But something is just…off. Lately, I've had this feeling when I'm with them, when I watch them interact. They've been best friends for practically their whole lives, so of course that means they're close. But lately, I've started to think that they might have more feelings for each other than they're letting on…or even than they know or are willing to admit."

Tyler's eyes shot up to his hairline. "What are we talking here? You think they could be sexually attracted to each other?"

I helped myself to another chip piled with guacamole to avoid saying anything incriminating and instead nodded.

Tyler pursed his lips. "Hmm. I don't know, babe, it might not be a good idea to rock the boat. If you say something, they could get pissed off—guys don't like you questioning their sexual orientation—as I've learned first-hand."

I shook my head and swallowed the bite of food. "I don't think they'd be mad at me for bringing it up." I thought back to my conversation with Sullivan where he freely admitted he'd had sexual experiences with guys in his younger years.

"Still, I don't think it's a good idea. On the other end of the spectrum, they could decide you're right and fall madly in love with each other and leave you by the wayside. It might turn out that women—and now you—have been a crutch for them this whole time. And if you help them heal, they might not need that crutch—need you—anymore."

My chest tightened. I hadn't ever considered that possibility. "If it came to that, I guess my sacrifice would be my way of showing my true love for them. And if that were to happen, as much as it would kill me, I know that it would be the right thing to do. I want happiness for Will and Sullivan more than I want it for myself."

Tears welled in my eyes as I spoke. I tried my best to keep them in, but when I looked at Tyler, the look on his face was so tender that one lone tear slipped down my cheek. I quickly dabbed it away with a napkin.

"Oh, honey. Come here."

He held out his arms and pulled me in for a hug. I let myself cry for a bit, allowing the full weight of what I'd just shared hit me. Will and Sullivan's happiness needed to come before my own, that much I was sure of.

When I pulled away, Tyler placed his hands on my shoulders. "If that's how you feel, then yes, you need to say something. But be gentle. Big, strong men like Will and Sullivan don't like having their masculinity questioned."

I nodded, dabbing at the corners of my eyes with my

fingertips. Gentle. Of course, I could do that. All I needed to do was sit them down for a serious talk. It wouldn't be easy—not in the slightest. But after discussing it with Tyler and knowing it'd been weighing on my mind for days on end, it was clear. The Talk needed to happen. Not just for my own sanity and peace of mind. But for Will and Sullivan's. I wanted to look at the positives that could come from this. *There would be positives, right?*

Tyler and I started walking back to the salon, stomachs full and minds clear. While I wasn't necessarily looking forward to The Talk, deciding to go through with it was giving me a newfound sense of purpose and direction. I felt like I was ready to take on the rest of my day.

Before we reached the salon, my phone started ringing. Pulling it out of my purse, I checked the screen. It was my mom. I gave Tyler an apologetic look, but he just shrugged.

"Answer it. Your next client won't be here for another twenty."

I nodded, mouthing a thank you as I pressed the accept button.

"Hi, Mom. How are you?"

"Hi, sweetheart. I'm doing well, what about you?"

"I'm good. What's up?"

"Well, I was just calling to invite you and your ..." Awkward pause. "Um, Sullivan and Will home for Thanksgiving."

I stopped in my tracks. Not exactly what I was expecting this call to be about.

"Are you sure? You want the three of us to be there? What about Dad?"

"You just leave your father to me. I'm missing my best girl and you're long overdue for a visit."

I sighed. She had a point. But already my stomach was churning. "Okay, sure, why not? I'll talk to the guys. I'd love to come home for Thanksgiving. It might be a good thing."

"That's the spirit. I can't wait to see you. And maybe I can teach Sullivan a thing or two about roasting the perfect Thanksgiving turkey."

We both laughed. My mother was making jokes about one of my ménage boyfriends? Not really something I ever thought would happen. Okay, then.

The two of us chatted some more, catching up with small talk before I had to go get ready for my next client. Once I hung up, I walked into the salon, a dumbfounded look on my face.

"How's your mama doing?" Tyler asked, sweeping up the last few bits of hair from his station.

"You'll never believe what just happened."

Tyler immediately stopped sweeping and his eyes snapped up to mine. "Spill."

I relayed the whole conversation to him, from my mom's invitation to her joke about cooking with Sullivan. And Tyler stood there, in disbelief.

"Is this a trap? It feels kind of like a trap." My heart was racing as a thousand different worries about the whole situation went speeding through my mind.

"Hon, who the hell knows? But if it seems like even one of your parents is on board with your threesome lifestyle, I say you do everything in your power to keep that good mojo going."

He was right. The fact that my mom was even a little

more open to my situation meant that my dad might be close to accepting it, too. The three of us had to show up to Thanksgiving, as loving and normal as ever, to show my family that this could work.

The only thing left to do was to convince Will and Sullivan to come with me to visit my gun-toting, ex-military, ultra-traditional father.

Piece of frickin' cake.

I guess our Talk would just have to wait.

Chapter Twenty-three

Sullivan

FROM THE MOMENT WE WALKED THROUGH THE DOOR, I could feel the tension in the air. We'd landed in Texas an hour ago, and rented a car for the drive to Adrienne's parents' house out in the country. It was a sprawling, one-story, ranch-style home with a metal roof and low, wooden fencing surrounding the vast property where a couple of dogs and chickens roamed freely. It was peaceful and serene. It was everything that none of us were feeling right now.

But now, standing in the foyer, my insides felt like they were being twisted by a fork, because standing across from us was Adrienne's father.

He was a tall man, with a silver crew cut and piercing blue eyes. Adrienne had warned us about the most important things: ex-military, gun enthusiast, ultra-traditional values. But even if she hadn't warned us, I would gather all that in an instant. His expression was stern as he looked between Will and me. But despite the grim, steely look in his eyes, he embraced Adrienne with open arms, clearly overjoyed to see her.

"I'm glad you're here," he told her, voice low. Betsey plastered on a tense smile and hugged Adrienne again.

Once they released her, Adrienne stepped back, and stood in between Will and me once again.

"Daddy, this is Sullivan. Sullivan, this is my father, Noah." She looked at me, meeting my eyes just briefly before a pink blush colored her cheeks. "And this is Will."

I wanted to take her hand, to reach over and touch her in some way, wanted to comfort her and promise that everything would okay. But the truth was, I had no idea if this would all turn out okay. Adrienne valued her family above all else, and that included her family's opinion of the man, or in this case, *men* she was dating.

Adrienne fidgeted nervously between us and I reached one hand out toward her father. "Pleased to meet you, sir. Thank you for having us in your home."

He grunted something that I wasn't sure were actual words, but returned my handshake with a firm grip.

He and Will exchanged a handshake next. "Nice to meet you, Mr. Edmonds. You've raised a wonderful daughter," Will said, his voice firm, and not nearly as nervous-sounding as mine.

Did he know something I didn't? Why was he so relaxed about this whole thing?

Betsey and Adrienne's eyes had flitted nervously between the three of us men, clearly worried about what his response to us would be. But after giving us both the once-over, Noah had nodded, his mouth in a thin, taut line, and retreated to what looked like a man cave around the corner from the living room.

I let out a deep breath and followed Adrienne and Betsey farther into the house.

Okay then.

In my mind, Thanksgiving was supposed to be about family coming together, people laughing and cooking together, each going around the table and saying what they were thankful for, at least that's the way I'd seen it portrayed in the movies.

Family holidays were something Will and I missed out on growing up. Sure, the local church came by the group home every year with some cold turkey and mashed potatoes, but even then, we knew it wasn't the real thing. But judging by the tense, awkward way Adrienne's parents couldn't even really look us fully in the eye, something told me our first family Thanksgiving was about to be more authentic than I realized—awkward family tension and all.

As Betsey gave us a tour of the house, the contractor in me couldn't help but take in every detail with a careful, attentive eye. You can learn a lot about a person based on their home, and I could tell Will and I had a lot to learn. Fast.

Antique guns hanging in a cabinet, animal heads mounted on the walls … I wasn't sure why I was also expecting to find a bomb shelter stocked with years' worth of food and supplies. Or maybe I was wishing I'd walk in on a home-distillery brewing up their own moonshine, because Lord knows I needed a strong drink right about now surrounded by guns and dead animals mounted to walls.

"This is Adrienne's room," Betsey said, opening the door to a large bedroom with pale pink walls and cheerleading trophies lined up across the top shelves. "Or at least it was. When she moved out, I couldn't bear to change very much of it. I guess part of me was always hoping she'd move right back in." Betsey let out a little laugh.

"Mom," Adrienne muttered, shaking her head with embarrassment. She crossed her arms as she walked slowly through her old room, her fingertips lingering on her old, fluffy pink comforter.

"It suits you," Will said, a small grin forming on his face.

"How long until the pink takes over our place, do you think?" I chimed in.

"Oh, I'm surprised it hasn't happened already," Betsey teased, looping her arm through Adrienne's. Adrienne smiled and shook her head again.

"I'm used to the guys ganging up on me, but Mom, you, too? Two I can handle, but three is too much."

Will and I laughed, but the joke hit too close to home for Betsey. She stayed silent, unable to hide the grimace passing over her face. She patted Adrienne's hand before letting go of her arm and walking out of the bedroom.

Will followed close behind Betsey, ready to ask distracting questions about the shiplap above the fireplace, while I hung back to check on Adrienne, whose face looked like it was on the verge of crumbling.

"Hey, baby, it's alright. Your joke just caught her off guard. She'll come around. They both will."

Adrienne sighed, tears welling up in her eyes as she looked up at me.

"But my dad has barely said two words to you guys since you got here. He didn't even join us for the tour."

"He's busy." I shrugged, wrapping my arm around her shoulders. "Cleaning his guns, maybe."

Adrienne laughed, playfully elbowing me in the ribs.

"No." She smiled, taking my hand and leading me out of the room. "Gun cleaning day is Sunday."

After we finished the tour, Betsey led us into the living room to meet Adrienne's brother who had just arrived.

Adrienne threw her arms around his neck, and then nudged him forward to come and meet me and Will.

All I knew was that his name was Finn, and he was a few years younger than Adrienne and was just finishing college. The kid was massive—built like his father with broad shoulders and a trim waist. His face lit up in a smile as he shook Will's hand and mine.

"Good to meet you guys."

"You, too," Will offered.

"If you guys are interested, after dinner, I've organized a game of flag football with a couple of buddies."

Adrienne laughed. "Oh, no, you don't. When Finn says flag football and a couple of buddies, what he means is his college buddies who are all NFL hopefuls and full-contact until someone's bleeding."

"Or has a broken bone," Betsey supplied.

Finn rolled his eyes. "That happened one time, Mom. And it was a jammed finger. It wasn't broken."

"Sounds like fun." I grinned.

"Count us in," Will added.

Adrienne let out a little sigh beside us and put her hand on her hip.

"Do you play for the university?" I asked.

Finn nodded and his face lit up. He spoke about his team's stats and the big game they were getting ready for next. It was obvious football meant a lot to him.

"Didn't Adrienne tell you? Finn's an excellent ball player. He's been invited to the league's pro day where scouts will look at him to play professionally."

My gaze darted to Adrienne, eyes wide. Her little brother might become a professional football player?

"That's incredible," I offered to Finn. "Congrats, man."

Adrienne only shrugged. "I don't know anything about football."

Her brother regarded the three of us together with an amused expression, like all of this was funny to him.

Will turned to Adrienne's mom. "Can we help you with anything in the kitchen, Betsey?"

She shook her head. "Everything's ready. Let's head into the dining room."

She called around the corner for Adrienne's father, who'd been avoiding us on the other side of the house since we arrived.

Mr. Edmonds sat at the head of the table, while Betsey sat at the other end. Finn and Adrienne sat at one side of the table, and Will and I sat across from them. After a short prayer, Mr. Edmonds began to carve the bird, and he didn't hesitate to start grilling me and Will.

"So, boys, Betsey tells me you two had a hard go of it growing up. In the foster care system, was it?" He didn't look at us as he spoke, but somehow his stare at the turkey while he ran the knife through it felt intentional.

"It was a group home, sir," Will replied. He kept his eyes trained on me as he spoke. It was a connection we shared, and one we didn't particularly like talking about.

"Orphans, right. So, family values weren't a large part of your upbringing."

Damn. That stung. Will and I paused, a silent moment of restraint passing between us.

"The nuns did their best," I said shortly.

"I see. And was it the nuns who taught you to share one woman between yourselves like a couple of wild animals fighting over a carcass?"

Fuck. I clenched my jaw, careful to keep the first thing that popped into my head from coming out of my mouth. We were there to be civil, to persuade Adrienne's parents that Will and I were the best men for her—and that there was nothing wrong with us coming as a package deal.

But right now? It was taking all the restraint in the world from telling him to fuck off and mind his business.

Across the table, Adrienne stiffened. Her eyebrows knitted together as she watched her father pass the plate of cut meat over to Finn.

"Respectfully, sir, that's not the kind of relationship we have with your daughter," I said, setting down the bowl of mashed potatoes that had been passed to me. I kept my voice level and calm. There was still hope for turning this around.

But Mr. Edmonds only chuckled—a humorless sound that came out flat. "You don't have a *relationship* with my daughter. I don't even know what to call this stupid little stunt you're pulling here, Adrienne, but it's over." Adrienne pressed her palms against the table. "Daddy…"

"Sir, if you'd allow us to explain—" Will started, but Mr. Edmonds cut him off.

"I don't want you to explain, I don't want to know

anything more about it. There is nothing more ridiculous than the idea of my one and only daughter being shared between two men like she's the last woman alive on Earth. It's disgusting and immoral and I won't stand for it. And you're living with them now? Honestly, Addy, after all your mother and I have done for you, after all the ways we've supported you, this is how you repay us?"

Adrienne's face crumpled with each word. It broke my heart to see her so upset by her father's refusal to understand, but more than anything, it was pissing me off. I could feel Will's body tensing in his chair next to me, and I could tell that Will was having trouble controlling his anger, too. Finn sat rigidly and quietly across the table.

"Noah, please," Betsey whispered from across the table, but he simply raised his hand to silence her and continued.

"She's our daughter, Betsey. And I won't let her be passed around between them like some floozy. It's not natural. It's not right."

That was the final straw. My skin boiling, I couldn't stop myself—or Will—from what happened next.

"Noah, I don't know what you think is happening

between your daughter and us, but I can assure you that it's nowhere near as 'unnatural' or 'wrong' as you think," I said, unable to keep the anger out of my voice.

"We love her," Will added, slamming his palm down on the table.

I waited for Adrienne to say something, to correct her father, to tell him that this was her decision, but instead, she stayed eerily quiet and stared straight ahead, refusing to meet our eyes.

But I couldn't stand by and stay quiet, not when something so important was on the line. I leaned in closer toward her father. "This little 'stunt', as you've called it, is three adults in a loving, consensual relationship. If you can't handle it, that's your problem."

With that I stood, and Will stood to join me. My chest was heaving, and Will's hands were curled into tight fists. We both stood there for a moment, our eyes trained on Adrienne's father, whose steely blue eyes stared back at us, eerily calm and focused.

I tried to look at Adrienne, but she wouldn't meet my gaze. She stared down at her hands, which were folded in her lap, tears on the brink of falling from her eyes.

"Fuck this," Will grunted, loudly pushing his chair back and marching out the front door. I followed him, ready to storm out of that house and never look back. But a small tug at my heart made me turn before I'd taken two steps.

I watched Adrienne from the doorway, waiting to see if she would leave with us, choose us over the family that clearly couldn't accept us. Tears rolled freely down her cheeks as she leaned across the table to comfort her mother, whose face was buried in one of her maroon embroidered napkins.

When she didn't turn to look at me, I knew she had made her decision. I followed Will to the front door and headed outside. I joined Will in the rental car and climbed inside.

"Fuck!" he roared, slamming his fist against the steering wheel.

We hadn't even been there long enough to unload our overnight bags from the car, which in hindsight, I guess, was a good thing. It meant we didn't have to go back inside. But then I realized that meant Adrienne's bag was still in the trunk, too. I climbed out and unlatched it, reaching inside to retrieve her rolling suitcase, and a small purple duffle bag that still smelled like her. I carried them to the front porch and set them down before turning for the car again.

Part of me hoped Adrienne would come rushing out the door, but the other part of me knew she wouldn't. That's just not how life worked—not for me any way. If life had taught me anything so far, it was that love wasn't in the cards for me.

"Let's get out of here," I said to Will.

He started up the car, and took off down the gravel driveway, sending up a plume of dust behind us.

With each mile down the road, the tension in my body only seemed to coil tighter. Will stayed silent beside me, and I knew he felt just as shitty.

It was an hour into the drive before he finally spoke. "I'm fucking starving."

I shook my head, realizing that we never got to enjoy a single bite of our first ever family Thanksgiving dinner. "Happy Thanksgiving."

He shot me a sidelong glance. "You too, man."

"What happens now?" I asked.

Will blew out a slow breath. "Don't know."

A few more miles ticked past in silence before either of us spoke again. I wondered if Will was replaying the words Adrienne's dad had spewed at us, and the way she sat there silently, refusing to look at us.

"Finn was cool," Will said at last.

"Do you think they know he's gay?"

He shook his head. "I don't even think he knows. How well do you think that would go over in that household?"

"Like a lead balloon."

"Exactly," he murmured.

A few minutes later we pulled into the airport to buy an overpriced flight home, and into a new, uncertain future, one that didn't include a woman we were both in love with.

Chapter Twenty-four

Adrienne

TEARS STREAMING DOWN MY CHEEKS, I watched Will and Sullivan storm out of my parents' home, feeling hurt and completely helpless.

My dad stared angrily at his plate, his jaw clenched and his hands flat on the table. I rose to comfort my mom who'd left the table and was sniffling quietly in the kitchen.

When she saw the look on my face, my mom reached her arms out to pull me in. And that's when I totally lost it.

I fell into my mom's arms, burying my face in her shoulder as the sobs poured out of me. It felt like I was in high school all over again, but instead of being heartbroken over some boy, this time it was so much more real—and so much worse.

"Oh, honey, it will be okay," she said, stroking my hair like she used to when I was little.

"I don't know if it will." I pulled back to look at her

face, hoping she would have something more comforting to say. But all she could do was look sadly right back at me and nod. My mom loved me, but she wasn't the kind of person to lie just to make me feel better. I knew she understood the gravity of this situation, and didn't know what to say any better than I did. The truth was, this might not be okay. It might not be something we could solve.

"I'll try talking to your father."

I huffed out a deep sigh, and leaned one hip against the counter as she stormed out of the kitchen.

From my spot in the kitchen, I could hear my mom's stern, hushed voice scolding my dad, as well as his frustrated voice angrily replying. I knew she'd get him to calm him down eventually, but when it came to changing his mind? That would take a miracle.

Carrying his half-eaten plate into the kitchen, Finn shot me a worried look. "How are you holding up?"

I shook my head, knowing that if I opened my mouth to speak, I'd just break down crying again.

"Come on," he urged, pouring me a glass of white wine, and urging me into the living room.

While my parents continued to argue, Finn ate his turkey at the table—some Thanksgiving this had turned out to be, and I took my glass of wine and curled up into a ball on the couch, distraught and exhausted. Tears continued to fall as I tried to figure out what to do next.

I knew that my dad was going to have a hard time accepting my new relationship, but I had no idea he would be so angry. Or that he'd make a scene in front of Will and Sullivan. Without my father's approval—or even a little bit of his acceptance—I wasn't sure if I'd be able to stay in this relationship at all. Knowing my relationship made my dad so upset killed me, but the thought of walking away from these two men I'd fallen so completely in love with killed me even more. I'd been through bad breakups before, but leaving Will and Sullivan? That would be a whole new level of broken I hadn't ever experienced.

A couple hours later, my dad still wasn't speaking to me, and I decided I needed to get out of here. My mom had tried to convince me to just stay at home with them, but I knew I needed someone else to talk to—and to not be around my disappointed father for any longer than necessary.

I decided I would fly back home and stay the night at Dani's.

When it was time to go, I hugged my parents and Finn goodbye, unable to ignore the grim look in my dad's eyes as I gathered my bags and walked away.

After an uneventful flight, Dani picked me up at the airport. Once I got in the car, she leaned over to hug me over the center console.

"You okay, girl?" Her expression said it all. I looked like shit. She was right. I knew my eyes were bloodshot from all the crying, my face puffy and red.

Tears welled up in my eyes again, and I bit my lip and nodded. "I just don't know what to do," I said after a long pause.

She nodded somberly. "Well, the good news is I've got a bottle of wine at home with our name on it."

We spent the rest of the ride to her place in relative silence. Dani vented to me a little bit about her own hectic Thanksgiving. Her mother-in-law insisted on judging every single dish Dani brought to the meal and scolded her at one point for letting the baby nap in the middle of the day. I nodded along and tried to listen and be empathetic, but my mind was still running a hundred miles an hour, trying to find a solution where I could stay with the men I loved without losing my relationship with my parents.

When we got to Dani's, I took a long, hot shower, hoping the steam and soap would clear my head. The shower felt amazing after a long and emotionally draining day, and after I changed into my pajamas, I was ready for some wine and girl talk.

Dani and I curled up on her couch, each tucked under our own fluffy blankets like we used to in high school. She insisted that I have something to eat, and a slice of uneaten pumpkin pie sat in my lap.

"Alright," Dani said, settling into her spot on the couch, "tell me everything that happened."

I took a long sip of wine and released a heavy exhale. Then I launched into my story, explaining every detail from the way my dad greeted the three of us when we walked through the door to the way Will and Sullivan stormed out after things got heated between them and my dad. Dani nodded along quietly, her eyes growing wide and worried at each twist and turn.

When I finished, she let out a low sigh. "Adrienne, I'm so sorry. That sounds about ten-thousand times worse than my Thanksgiving. Have you talked to the guys yet?"

I shook my head.

"I guess I just didn't realize that my dad would react so strongly. I knew it would be a lot for him to process, but I thought that after all these months he would have processed it more. And at least been able to play nice at the dinner table. But I guess I was wrong."

"Your poor mom. There's no way she would have invited you guys if she thought that would happen. She must feel awful."

"She was so upset. And so were Will and Sullivan before they stormed out. I've never seen them angry like that before. Part of me was flattered. They were ready to fight tooth and nail to defend what we have. But the more I think about it, the more I think that maybe I was wrong about this whole thing."

Dani frowned. "What do you mean?"

"Three people in one relationship? What the hell was I thinking? There's a reason more people don't do it. It's messy and complicated. There's no way it can work."

"But what about all their great qualities? All you've ever told me about them is how amazing each man is on his own—and how even more amazing they are together. Are you really willing to let that go?"

I sighed, tucking my still damp hair behind one ear. "These past couple months have been amazing, sure. But the more I think about it, the more I can't help but wonder if it was all a fantasy, a dream."

I paused and sucked in a deep breath. It broke my heart to say the next words, but I knew I had to get them out.

"And after how today went with my parents, I'm starting to think it might be time for me to wake up."

Chapter Twenty-five

Sullivan

"Too much," Will grunted, shaking his head at the brightly colored balloon and flower arrangement I'd pulled up online.

I nodded and kept scrolling. "You're right. I just want to make sure that whatever we do, it's enough."

It had been a couple days since the Thanksgiving disaster. Adrienne had texted to say she was staying at Dani's, and Will and I had spent every second since leaving her parents' house trying to figure out how to get her back.

"Maybe not flowers," he said, rubbing the back of his neck. "Too cliché. Plus, we've already done that."

"It needs to be meaningful, something she can't resist. She's the one. I've known it since the moment we first met her, and I'll be damned if I don't do everything in my power to win back our girl."

Will nodded. I knew he thought I was being overemotional when we first met Adrienne, but I could tell that after everything we'd been through with her, he felt the same way I did. Even if he wouldn't say it out loud.

Finishing off the last swallow of his morning coffee, Will put his mug in the sink. He began pacing around the kitchen, something he did when he really needed to think.

I kept scrolling online, trying to find the perfect gift to show Adrienne just how much we care. It had to be something more than the usual chocolates or flowers. This wasn't any grand gesture for any girl. This was our one chance to make sure Adrienne knew just how goddamn serious we were about her.

Suddenly, it hit me. I knew exactly what to do.

Pulling my phone out of my pocket, I started dialing, waving Will over to join me at the table.

He raised an eyebrow at me and shook his head. "What are you doing?"

I cocked my head to the side, sucking in air with a low hiss.

"Hope you're ready to be diplomatic as fuck."

***

That night Will and I prepared the house for our grand gesture to win Adrienne over for good. She'd agreed to come over and talk with us, but she made it clear that our relationship was still up in the air. It stung to hear the words come out of her mouth, but hearing her hesitancy just made me want to fight even harder.

Will and I both showered and changed into suitable date-night attire. For me, that meant dark jeans and a gray Henley. For Will, it meant jeans and his nice black t-shirt.

Even though we'd initially decided against it, we still went ahead and bought a flower arrangement for the hallway table near the front door. Twenty-four long-stem red roses, one dozen from each of the men who loved her. The roses were only part of the gesture. What we had planned would really blow her away. At least, that was our intention.

The doorbell rang a few minutes after seven, and Will and I walked together to answer it. We opened the door to find Adrienne standing there with a hesitant look on her face, her curves perfectly wrapped up in a pair of skinny jeans and a pale yellow silk top.

"You look beautiful," I said as Will and I leaned

down to kiss each of her cheeks at the same time.

"Gorgeous, as always," Will added.

Adrienne smiled, but it didn't quite reach her eyes. It was hard for her to be with us when she was still so torn about our relationship.

"Thanks, guys." Her eyes widened when she saw the roses in the hall. "Are those for me?"

"The first of many surprises," I said, ushering her through the door and shutting it behind her.

We followed her into the kitchen, where her favorite bottle of white was waiting in an ice bucket on the counter. She smiled weakly when she saw the wine, taking a glass from Will as he poured it for her.

"Guys…" she started, the look of hesitation only growing.

"There's more," Will cut her off and led her into the dining room.

We'd set the dining table with our best flatware, and on it, we'd tracked down all the food from our first dates. Chicken tacos from McGilley's pub where we first met her, dumplings and spring rolls from the food truck on our first solo date, and containers of the homemade pasta from the Italian place Will took her to on their solo date. It was a lot of food—too much, probably—but hey, they didn't call it a grand gesture for no reason. But this wasn't the main surprise, and I couldn't wait to tell her what it was.

Adrienne stifled a gasp when she saw the table, staring with her hand clasped over her mouth at the spread.

"Are those...?" she said, pointing at the tacos.

Will and I nodded.

"And the food truck?"

I nodded again.

"The Italian place?"

Will smiled.

"You guys...this is...way too much food."

The three of us laughed, and I handed Adrienne a plate.

"We wanted to surprise you," I said.

"Are you hungry, sweetheart?" Will murmured, voice

hopeful.

She raised one shoulder, still appraising the table. "I could eat."

As she began to serve herself, Will and I exchanged a look. So far, things were going well. But there was no telling if our gesture would actually work.

We all sat down and dug in, the memories of our first dates almost as delicious as the food. We chatted lightly while we ate, asking Adrienne about Dani and the baby, each of us anticipating the verdict that was still yet to come.

Adrienne picked at her food, trying a little bit of everything, but really not giving any indication on what she was thinking.

When we finished eating, Will and I cleared the plates while Adrienne watched us from the kitchen counter. Her smile from dinner had faded, and it was clear the reality of our situation was hitting her all over again.

"This was very sweet and thoughtful of you both," Adrienne said. "Thank you for that."

"But?" Will stared at her, his eyes dark and concerned.

"But my parents. Thanksgiving was a disaster, and I can't just sweep that under the rug. If being with you two means losing them, I don't know if I can stay in this relationship."

"You're an adult now, sweetheart. Your parents don't rule your decisions. And it's clear they love you. If this is really what you want, they'll get over it."

Adrienne frowned. "Easy for you to say … you don't have parents."

Fuck. Low blow, babe.

Will and I stood silent, our faces stone. Immediately, Adrienne's face crumpled, shock and horror washing over her face.

"I'm so sorry, that was cruel of me. I'm just so confused, I don't know what to do. Losing you…losing my father…I feel like no matter what I choose, I lose."

I nodded. It was time to bring out the big guns. "We called your dad."

"You what?" she asked, voice high with surprise.

"We were able to smooth things over," Will said.

Adrienne's eyes widened, her whole face lighting up.

"Really? What did he say? What did you say to him?"

"He's willing to see our side," I said, moving closer to Adrienne. "Now that he knows how much we mean to you. And what you mean to us."

She jumped up and threw her arms around us, kissing both of our faces and hopping around excitedly. Adrienne squealed again, squeezing her arms tighter around us. "You two are amazing. I can't believe you did that. I talked to my mom this afternoon, she didn't say anything."

"We asked her to let us be the ones to surprise you," I admitted.

"My mom was in on it, too?" she asked.

Will and I only smiled.

She continued to praise us and shower us with kisses until her excitement turned into something slower and deeper. We moved to the bedroom, Will and I carrying her together and placing her down on the bed. We worked our mouths over each side of her neck while she unbuttoned both our jeans at the same time.

The three of us paused before moving any further, each of us exchanging a knowing look. Regular three-way sex was one incredible thing. Make-up sex three-way? Whole other ball game.

Chapter Twenty-six

Adrienne

MY WORK DAY WENT BY in a breeze. I only had a few clients, and they were all regulars, so the cuts I did were pretty routine, and our conversations were light and easy. Which meant that I had plenty of mental and emotional strength left to prepare for The Talk.

Now that things with my dad had been smoothed over, I felt like I was finally in a place with Will and Sullivan where we could finally have that conversation. Or at least try to. For as much as I loved chatting with Tyler and my regulars at work, I couldn't ignore the butterflies floating around my stomach all day—or the buzzing anxieties in the back of my mind.

When I got home, I was greeted with kisses from my favorite guys and a glass of perfectly chilled white wine. Sullivan had made some yummy lemon chicken, and the three of us sat down and ate dinner together at the same table where just a few days before, I had been ready to walk away from this relationship.

Funny how things can change so quickly—just like

that.

"Sull, that chicken was incredible," I sighed, setting my fork down after taking my last bite.

"Don't know how you do it," Will added, smiling and shaking his head.

"I cook better when things in my life are good. So, I guess it's about time for me to quit contracting and open my own restaurant." Sullivan and I laughed, but Will just gave him a sour look.

Sullivan elbowed Will in the ribs. "Oh, come on, you know I'd make you my sous chef."

Will elbowed him back, which started a play fight between the two of them. It made me smile to watch them interact like this with each other, so open and happy and willing to touch each other's bodies. It felt like a glimpse into the life they could have with each other…which is why I decided right then and there that we needed to have The Talk. As soon as possible.

I began clearing our plates and cleaning up as the guys continued teasing each other. The butterflies in my stomach were fluttering at full force, and I went over the main points I wanted to get across to them in my head.

The memory of Tyler's voice warning me not to rock the boat surfaced in my mind, but I just pushed it away. These men meant everything to me—even more so now that I knew they were willing to fight for me. And what kind of woman would I be if I wouldn't do the same for them?

"Need any help?" Sullivan appeared by my side, ready to do whatever I needed.

I shook my head. "Actually, I was hoping the three of us could have a little chat. Why don't you and Will grab the bottle of wine and meet me on the couch."

Sullivan cocked his head, a curious look on his face. "Whatever you say, babe."

He kissed the top of my head and left to do what I'd asked him to.

I finished up the last of the dishes and met them at the couch. Will was sitting with his back straight, a tense, uneasy look on his face. Sullivan looked slightly more relaxed, but I could tell he was worried, too.

Placing myself strategically between them, I sat down and put a comforting hand on both of them.

"What's on your mind, sweetheart?" The concern in Will's voice was enough to break my heart then and there.

"It's nothing to be worried about. Well, not exactly nothing, because here I am, sitting you down and telling you there's something I want to talk about."

My heart was racing, and I couldn't seem to get my thoughts in order. What if what I had to say ruined everything? What if I offended them so much they left me for good? What if I didn't offend them and they left me for each other? Oh God, maybe this was a huge mistake.

I pulled a deep breath into my lungs.

"Babe, you know you can tell us anything. We're here for you. And we've already been through a lot together. Whatever it is, I'm sure it's not as scary as it feels in your head."

I took a big gulp of wine and let out a sigh. Here goes nothing …

"Lately, I've been noticing something between you two, and I don't know how aware you are of it yourselves."

I looked up, hoping they would have caught my drift already, but Will and Sullivan just stared at me blankly. Okay, then. I guess I'd have to be more direct.

"I think the two of you have feelings for each other."

Will scoffed, shaking his head in disbelief. Sullivan just stared at me, waiting for me to go on.

"When the three of us are in the bedroom, I can just feel it. You're both so careful not to touch each other, but I see the tension between you. I see it in the way one of you watches me take the other one in my mouth. Or the glances you share when the three of us are being intimate. I think you're both open for more, more than you realize—and not just with me, but with each other."

We sat in silence, and I watched as Will's jaw clenched and unclenched. He was processing, but he didn't look very happy. Sullivan, on the other hand, looked more neutral. Pensive, even.

Finally, it was Will who broke the silence.

"Sweetheart, I don't know where this is all coming from. Me and Sull aren't gay. We're not attracted to each other like that."

He turned to Sullivan, but he wasn't so quick to agree.

"Unless there's something I'm missing here, Sull?"

Sullivan rubbed his temples with his forefingers, exhaling slowly.

"Will, I love you. I've loved you since I was thirteen. My dick gets confused sometimes."

Shock spread across Will's face.

"And that means you're attracted to me?"

"Yeah, I think I am."

I couldn't believe what I was hearing. I was right. I'd been right all along. There was something between them. I didn't know whether to laugh or to cry.

"Look," I said, taking them both by the hand and guiding them to the master bedroom, "I know we have a rule that nothing sexual happens unless it's all three of us, but I'm going out with Dani tonight. I think it'd be good for you guys to stay in to talk...and explore whatever this is between you."

Before they could respond, I pushed them into the bedroom and closed the door behind them.

"Hey, really not cool, babe." Sullivan's muffled voice called out from behind the door.

"Figure this out," I replied, quickly gathering my

things to go to Dani's. "Goodbye. Love you."

Chapter Twenty-seven

Sullivan

"WHAT THE FUCK'S UP with Adrienne? She's crazy to think that…" Will stopped talking as I crossed the bedroom to face him.

Adrienne had closed us in here to "talk" and had left the house for the evening, hopeful that we could sort this out.

But so far? Will was being anything but cooperative. He could deny it all he wanted, but Adrienne knew the truth, and now so did I. It was staring me straight in the face. Well, almost.

"You're hard," I said, voice coming out soft.

He sucked in a breath and closed his eyes. "Dick's confused. That's all."

I didn't believe him. If he wanted to tell himself that his junk was merely overreacting on the off-chance that sex with our girl was on the table later, he could lie to himself all he wanted. Didn't mean I was going to buy it. Not in a million years.

"I don't believe you," I whispered.

He frowned, but his gaze dropped down to the front of my jeans, which were now sporting an obvious bulge, too.

"So, what the fuck does it matter?" He stalked across the room. "We've been best friends for two decades. Never once has anything happened."

But that was another lie. "That's not entirely true."

He blew out a frustrated breath.

I crossed the room and sat down on the edge of his bed. Will remained rooted in place, gazing out the window at the crescent moon and its ominous glow.

"Watching porn together a couple of times and jacking off when we were teenagers doesn't count as being gay," he said, still refusing to meet my eyes.

"I'm not saying we're gay."

"Bi—whatever."

I couldn't believe he couldn't just admit this. After all of his bravado with Adrienne about not worrying what others would think and now this. There was no one here to judge us. And it was just us—left alone to figure this shit out once and for all, and he couldn't even be honest with himself, with me.

"Newsflash, Will. It wasn't the porn that got me off back then. It was the sight of you—your cock so stiff and swollen. Knowing your eyes would occasionally drift over to where my hand worked on my own hard shaft. I'd never come so hard in my entire life."

At my admission, Will turned. His dark gaze was almost pained. "But you never..."

"Said anything? I know. I couldn't. Couldn't risk it ruining our friendship."

Understanding crossed over his features and he gave a tight nod. The first honest reaction I'd seen out of him all night. Back then, we only had each other. Two orphans who'd banded together. I wasn't about to let something like confused or misplaced sexual attraction get in the way of the only friend, hell, the only family I'd ever had.

"Don't get me wrong, I fucking adore the female body equally, man." I was quick to draw that definitive line in the sand myself.

And the more years we spent denying our attraction, the easier it became to stuff it down and hide it away, to make it all about the woman we were with. And I did love women. That was never a lie. They were beautiful. Maybe it made me a sexual deviant, a freak. But I wanted it all— the soft curves of a woman, accompanied with the hard, masculine planes of a man.

"Can I ask you something?" I asked.

He nodded, still watching me as though he was really seeing me for the first time.

"Have you ever messed around with a guy before?"

He shook his head.

It was what I expected him to say.

He swallowed, his throat bobbing. God, he was so damn sexy. So brooding and intense and masculine. Broad shoulders, five-o'clock shadow along his jaw, and even shooting this pissed-off vibe, there was no denying my attraction to him. "You?" he asked.

I nodded. "A couple of blow jobs when I was younger. That's about it."

If this information surprised Will, he didn't let on. "Why didn't you ever say anything?"

I shrugged. "Like I said, couldn't risk losing you. My

silence ensured our future, man, and I'd rather share you with a woman than not have you at all."

He took a step closer to the bed. "That won't happen."

I rose to my feet and stalked closer to him. Will remained rooted in place, watching me.

"Not even if I do this?" I leaned in close, bringing my mouth close to his. For a moment, time stopped. I thought he might pull away or give me a hard shove back onto my ass, but he didn't. I was over six feet tall, but Will still had a few inches on me, and at least a couple dozen pounds of muscle. If he wanted space, he wouldn't have even had to ask. He would have pushed, and I would have stepped back, and that would have been the end of it. Case closed.

Except ... he didn't.

Instead, his breathing grew uneven, and his pulse hammered almost violently in his throat.

Lifting up to accommodate our height difference, I brought my mouth to his, placing a damp kiss against his parted lips. Will didn't respond. He didn't return the kiss, but he didn't push me away either.

It was a start.

"Don't lie to yourself. Or to me." Gathering my courage, I placed my hand over the bulge in his jeans, stroking the massive length I knew he was hiding. His cock was stiff, and it bucked beneath my touch.

"*Jesus*," he grunted.

I'd seen him naked so many times, knew the look of his cock almost as well as I did my own. But I didn't know how he liked to be touched. Whether he'd want my fist pumping fast and hard, or in long, slow pulls. I knew that when Adrienne brought her mouth to him, he let her pleasure him with soft flicks of her tongue. Gentle caresses that teased. But I couldn't help but wonder if things would be different if I were the one on my knees before him. Imagining his hips pumping, his cock pressing urgently into the back of my throat, the palm of his hand on the back of my neck as he fucked my throat, fast and rough. It was enough to make my own cock weep with anticipation.

"I know you want this," I murmured, nipping at his mouth again.

"And if I don't?" His voice was almost painfully

tense against my own lips. Deep and stern, and so fucking sexy.

I shrugged. "Then you don't. And nothing changes between us. We will always be best friends and share our future with Adrienne, plain and simple."

Will's gaze zeroed in on mine. The electricity zapping between us could have short-circuited entire cities. Fuck, maybe entire counties.

"I mean it," I continued. "Either we do this, or we don't. But I won't let sex come between us. We're family. Us and Adrienne. I have everything I could ever want in you two, and that won't change."

He nodded, and I could see the exact moment he decided he believed me. His eyes flashed with understanding and then something darker—something more carnal. *Lust.*

Will gave me that shove I'd been expecting earlier, but this time when my back struck the wall, he was right there with me—pressing his firm, muscled chest to mine and taking my mouth in a hungry kiss. We sparred that way—hands groping, mouths fighting for control—tongues dueling until I was breathless and so fucking horny I could hardly stand it.

I gave an experimental thrust of my hips into his so that our cocks rubbed together, and Will let out a groan.

"That feels," he murmured, before stopping himself.

From my standpoint, *good* was too tame a word for what I felt. It felt incredible. Mind-altering. Life changing to be standing here with him, doing this.

I went back to kissing him, simply because I could. I'd waited so many years for this moment, always telling myself it could never happen. I wouldn't let it happen. Wouldn't risk it. But now it was happening, and it was even better than I'd ever imagined it could be.

I grabbed onto his jaw, running my fingers through his hair, but Will decided that was too much, and pushed my hands away from him, pinning my wrists to the wall above my head.

My heart hammered wildly in my chest. Everything about this was new and exciting. The jockeying for position, the physicality of it, the push and pull. I could feel him fighting it, even if his body wanted it—wanted me, he wasn't going to be easy to conquer, and I liked that even more.

I pressed my hips against his again, our cocks straining for each other's even through our jeans.

"What happens next?" he asked. His voice was deep and husky and filled with need. It drove me wild to know that I was the one getting him this way.

"What do you want to happen next?"

He was going to have to be abundantly clear. With words. Because I wasn't about to assume that after decades of living a relatively straight life that my best friend suddenly wanted me to fuck him.

"Take out my cock," he grunted.

It was the last thing I expected him to say. I tugged my wrists out of his grasp, and happily obliged, unbuttoning his jeans and tugging down the zipper. Soon Will had ripped his t-shirt off over his head, and I'd done the same. And then jeans were kicked off and boxers shoved down and we were back to kissing, our naked cocks rubbing gloriously together.

The weight of his dick in my hand felt both foreign and familiar, and I immediately liked it way too much. In long pulls I stroked him, working my hand up and down over his swollen shaft.

"Shit, that feels…"

His eyes closed, and his head dropped back. I loved doing this for him, loved being the one to make him feel good. But it still wasn't enough.

"Touch me," I ordered.

This was it. The moment of truth. He would either obey my command, or chicken the fuck out over the thought of jacking another man's cock. Please let it be the former, I prayed.

Will's knuckles grazed over my lower abdomen, tickling over the fine hairs I kept neatly groomed. Both of our gazes lowered to where he fisted my cock, and gave an experimental tug.

Fuck.

I couldn't believe Will was touching my cock. During all our years enjoying threesomes, he'd always ignored my dick with almost laser-focus. And now, here he was, wrapping it in his rough, calloused palm and giving it another pull. I grunted, my knees almost buckling at how good it felt. So unlike anything I'd ever felt with a woman. His pace was faster, harsher, his hand rough.

Sharing the same anatomy was a clear advantage. He

knew what felt good, what I'd enjoy, and all the ways to touch me. It bonded us on some deeper level.

"Fuck, Sullivan," he groaned. He gazed down at where he held me. My gaze followed. Even with his large hand, his fist didn't wrap all the way around.

Yes, I was hung. But it's not like he wasn't. Where my cock was long and straining upward to my belly button, his was thick and heavy, and even erect, jutted straight out in front of him, as though seeking my body heat.

"That's going to be inside you," I whispered, bringing my lips to his again.

Instead of returning my kiss, he bit my lower lip, causing it to sting. "The hell it will. In that scenario, I would be the top."

"That so?" I teased his cock, smearing the precum that had leaked out over the head with my thumb.

He sucked in a sharp inhale.

I pumped him in slow strokes, wanting to savor this, even though my entire body pulsed with an almost uncontrolled need. I was jacking Will's cock and I fucking loved it.

Angling my body even closer, I placed one hand around both of our cocks. Will's hand dropped away as he looked down at us in wonder, pupils blown, eyes wide as he gazed at the erotic sight of our cocks rubbing together.

I experimented, stroking my hand up and down over us both.

"Fuck. That feels good."

Damn straight it did. I've fantasized about this exact moment for, oh, I don't know, fifteen years. It was even better than I could have imagined.

His stubble scraped my own as his mouth found mine again.

"You going to suck it, or are you just going to jack me all night?" he asked, his tone slightly cocky.

For how resistant he was, Will was catching on damn quick.

He wouldn't have to ask me twice. Treating our cocks to a final stroke, I released us.

With my heart hammering in my throat, I lowered myself to my knees. I fisted his cock, then jacked it once, slowly, savoring the solid feel of him in my fist. Then I brought it to my mouth, sucking him deep, almost to the base.

"Holy fuck," he cursed and thrust his hips experimentally, pumping his cock in and out of my throat.

He was making me totally crazy, and this was going so much better than I ever dreamed. Had he wanted this, fantasized about it like I had all those years?

I looked up, and was shocked to find him watching me. I thought maybe he'd pretend I was Adrienne— pretend that it was her pretty mouth he was fucking and not mine. But then Will's fingers sank into my hair, and he let out another low groan.

"Sully."

My name on his lips melted the last bit of my heart. I gripped his shaft with one hand, stroking what I couldn't fit into my mouth. My free hand grasped his balls lightly and Will made a choked sound of pleasure. Something in between a cry and a shout, and I decided I'd never heard a more erotic sound in all my life. I loved that I was pleasuring him, that it was me he was losing control for.

My cock hung heavily between my legs, leaking

precum, but I ignored it. The only thing I cared about was making Will come, giving him even one ounce of the pleasure he was giving me by giving in to this moment. If I could have suspended time and stayed here for all of eternity, I would have. Rugburn on my knees, painfully swollen erection—none of it mattered. He was the only thing of importance right now.

"Fuck, Sullivan." He cursed again, his hips picking up speed. "You're going to make me come."

"That's kind of the point." I grinned up at him, before licking along the vein that snaked along the side of his thick shaft.

He made another wordless sound of pleasure. I could have done this all night, learning what he liked, bringing him right to the brink before backing off again. I would have done so gladly.

"You like doing that?" he asked, tangling his hands in my hair.

I shrugged, my mouth occupied. "Your dick likes me," I finally managed.

"Fuck yes, it does." He thrust forward, pressing himself all the way to the back of my throat.

Will gazed down at me while I worked, either not caring that it was a dude blowing him, or just enjoying the fact it was me. I had no idea which. I didn't care. With his long shaft in my mouth, with his sexy grunted sounds, I was so far gone it didn't matter anymore.

"Finish me," he grunted.

"Gladly." I increased my speed, pumping him faster while continuing to suck the broad head of him.

"Gonna come now," he warned.

I don't know if he expected me to pull away, but fuck that. I did no such thing. Gripping his base with both hands, I stroked while he emptied himself down my throat. It was salty and bitter, and perfect. It was Will. The man I'd loved for as long as I could remember.

"That was…" He scrubbed a hand through his hair, gazing down at me with something like admiration.

I rose to my feet and shoved him down onto the mattress. "My turn."

We laid side by side on the mattress, kissing for a long time. Will's cock laid semi-hard on his belly, and my hard shaft was currently wrapped in his palm where he treated it to long, firm strokes that seemed engineered specifically to make me lose my mind.

"You like it?" he asked.

"Too much."

His mouth descended onto mine again, and while he sucked on my tongue, I came all over his hand and my belly.

Tonight had been incredible and I prayed this wasn't both the first and last time we enjoyed each other's bodies.

After we cleaned up in the bathroom, we fell back onto the bed. "What do you think Adrienne's doing?" he asked.

I could have laughed. It was the exact thought drifting through my brain at the moment. "She's at Dani's," I said.

"Let's call her. I'm ready for her to come home."

"Me, too," I said, reaching for my cell phone on the nightstand.

"We gonna tell her?" he said.

"No secrets, right?" I asked.

He grunted something that I was sure was a reply, but what it meant, I wasn't sure.

Chapter Twenty-eight

Adrienne

"HELLO?" I CALLED, unlocking the front door and wandering inside to the living room. The lamp on the table kept the room softly lit, but there were no other signs of life. I'd stayed away most of the evening, bringing Chinese food and a chick-flick over to my best friend Dani's house for a girls' night in. Since she'd had her daughter, we were way overdue, but as fun as it was, I had been so distracted through much of the movie that I couldn't even tell you how it ended.

"In here, babe," Sullivan's voice called from the bedroom.

My heart picked up speed as I headed toward his voice. I slipped off my shoes and tossed my purse onto the couch before entering the master bedroom. The sight greeting me was a welcome one, so why was my stomach knotted with nerves?

Will and Sullivan were sprawled across the massive bed, looking content and relaxed. Part of me expected World War III to erupt when I'd challenged them earlier.

But judging by their demeanor, there was no blood or broken bones. Will was dressed in a pair of sweatpants, no shirt, his feet bare. His face was guarded, but his posture was relaxed, and he was lounging against the pillows that were propped against the headboard.

Sullivan was wearing a white t-shirt and a pair of loose-fitting gym shorts. His hair was mussed, and he looked happy and comfortable lying across from Will. They weren't touching, weren't doing anything to give me any indication if something went down tonight, but still, something in the air around us felt different.

Placing one knee on the end of the bed, I hoisted myself up and crawled toward them as butterflies danced around in my belly. So many questions. There were so many questions on the tip of my tongue that my brain threatened to short-circuit. "Well?" was all I could get out.

Sullivan's mouth twitched with a smile, and he patted the place in between them. "Come here. Get comfortable."

I obeyed, crawling to the spot between them, still studying them closely. Had something happened? Would they tell me if it had?

My stomach tightened with nerves. What if Tyler was right? What if they decided they were in love with each and that there was no room for me in this relationship?

But then Sullivan took my hand, lacing his fingers with mine. "How was your girls' night?"

The tension in my shoulders relaxed immediately. Leave it to Sullivan to be thinking about me, and my night, and how I was doing versus the monumental thing that maybe had just happened between him and Will.

God, I loved him so much it hurt.

"It was fine. I got to see Dani and the baby." My voice sounded tight. "How did everything go here?" My gaze darted over to Will.

His expression gave nothing away, but he stroked my arm lightly with the back of his knuckles.

The guys traded a curious look that I had no idea what it meant, but left Sullivan smirking.

"Just dandy," Will said at last.

"Wow. Dandy?" It wasn't a word I'd even known was in Will's vocabulary. "Somebody got their dick sucked." The words were blurted from my mouth before I could censor them.

Sullivan chuckled, and Will didn't deny it.

That strange tightness in my belly was back, but this time, rather than it being due to nerves, it was raw excitement.

I put my hands on Will's chest, leaning closer as a smile overtook my face. "Are you serious?"

Will nodded, lips turning up in a slight smile.

Sullivan punched him in the arm and Will's smile transformed into something even more beautiful.

"Oh my God. Tell me everything." I bounced on my knees on the bed, suddenly giddy with excitement.

Sullivan chuckled. "Patience, baby. First, how are you feeling about all this?"

"Are you mad?" Will asked.

"Mad? Not at all. I love you both, and I knew from day one of meeting you how much love you had for one another. I had only a hunch that you may someday explore that in a physical way, too."

"So you were basically just waiting for this moment?" Will asked, mouth still curved into a smile.

"I wouldn't say that. But over time I started to wonder if you just needed a gentle nudge."

Still holding my hand, Sullivan pressed our palms together tighter. I knew what this meant to him. I was pretty sure he'd been in love with Will for two decades. And I knew Will loved him back, in his own way. And now that it was all out in the open—it was like we could all breathe.

Will's expression said everything. It was so loving, so brave, and I felt all melty inside.

"My big, sexy, brave men. I love you so much." I pressed a soft kiss to each of their lips. "Now tell me more."

Sullivan smiled and cupped my face in his hands. "Our sexy, amazing, brave girl. Thank you for loving us, for showing us what true love feels like."

"You sure you feel okay?" Will asked.

"I think it's really fucking hot and I can't wait to see you both in action. I want a play by play so bad, but I'm trying to be respectful."

Sullivan broke into happy laughter. "There will be time for that later."

Will swallowed, a tight knot in his throat as he met my eyes. "You're incredible, sweetheart. I have no idea how we got here, but fuck. I've never felt this …"

He paused there, but I knew exactly what he meant.

This loved.

This accepted.

This free.

This happy.

Sullivan pressed a kiss to my forehead and tucked my hair behind one ear. "I don't want there to be any jealousy. Just like Will and I did all those years ago, I think we should establish some ground rules."

"Ground rules?" I shifted closer, getting comfortable between them.

Will played with one hand, tracing my life-lines while Sullivan held the other firmly in his hand.

"Just some boundaries so that lines don't get crossed and feelings don't get hurt," he continued.

I nodded.

"Probably a good idea," Will chimed in. "For instance, Sullivan and I have always had an agreement that we share in the truest sense of the word—that we don't have one-on-one time without each other present."

"But Sull and I did mess around that first night," I asked, confused.

Will nodded. "Yeah, but I told him if he fucked you, I'd punch him in the balls."

Sullivan laughed. "True story."

"So no going behind each other's backs," I said, nodding.

"Exactly," Will said.

"I can handle that," Sullivan said. His expression said so much more though. He looked so happy and loved and my heart threatened again to burst from happiness.

"Me, too," I wholeheartedly agreed to this new dynamic of our relationship.

"Come here, sweetheart," Will said. I curled against his chest, letting my eyes fall closed. "You too, Sully," Will added, his arms going around both of us in a way that felt new and familiar all at the same time, and incredibly right.

Chapter Twenty-nine

Adrienne

"SO, WILL, how are the fajitas?" I peered at him over the top of my margarita, trying to sound cheerier than usual.

He barely looked up at me in between bites. "Fine," he muttered.

I kept staring at him, hoping he'd make eye contact with me and flash a smile. When he barely looked up, I gave up and turned my attention to Sullivan.

"What about you, Sull? How are the shrimp tacos?"

He nodded and forced a smile before it quickly dissolved from his face, and the three of us returned to the tense silence that had been hanging between us for the entire evening.

My heart sank. I had been so excited to try the trendy new Mexican restaurant that had just opened around the corner from our house, but clearly, I was missing something. Will and Sullivan had been stiff and awkward from the moment I got home from work, but I had no idea what could be bothering them. As far as I was concerned, we'd never been closer. So why were they suddenly keeping something from me?

Ever since they had finally admitted to themselves that they had feelings for each other, things between us had been amazing, mind blowing, in fact. The sex was better than ever, and now that the emotional connection between Will and Sullivan was fully open and revealed, the affection between the three of us was almost overwhelming. And that's what made the awkwardness of this dinner so obvious. Something major was off. I just had no idea what. And clearly, Will and Sullivan weren't about to fill me in.

"Either of you want to try a bite of this?" I gestured to my plate, feeling silly, almost desperate trying to get them to open up and act normal. But I wasn't about to roll over and let this dinner pass without trying.

"I'm okay," Sullivan said, pushing some Spanish rice around his plate with his fork.

"All you," Will added.

The two of them exchanged a look I couldn't quite decipher, and suddenly, I couldn't ignore the pit forming in my stomach.

It must be me. There was no other explanation. I thought that things were going well between the three of us since they admitted their feelings for each other, but maybe I was wrong. Maybe they'd been pretending with me the whole time. Maybe as time went on, they'd actually realized how much more they love each other than they love me and were just waiting until I was full of tacos and margaritas to let me down gently.

Tears welled in my eyes, and my heart started pounding in my chest. I couldn't bear the thought of almost losing them, just when I thought everything was perfect. We'd had *The Talk*, we'd set some ground rules, but maybe none of that was enough. Maybe our little experiment in ménage was the last one they needed before they decided they didn't need a woman in their lives anymore. Suddenly, it dawned on me that this might be my last date with Will and Sullivan. Ever.

Appetite now gone, I gently pushed my plate away. Then I downed the rest of my drink and spent the rest of dinner mentally preparing for them to break up with me at the end of the night.

When we got home, I marched straight to the bedroom and got ready for bed. If they were going to break up with me out of the blue, it was on them to sit me down and start the conversation. There was no way I'd let myself be a sitting duck, just waiting for them to break my heart and end the most amazing, fulfilling relationship I'd ever been in forever. I was done pushing them to talk. They'd do it when they were good and ready.

I slipped into my favorite silk pajama set and went to the bathroom to brush and floss my teeth. A few minutes into my routine, Will and Sullivan appeared in the doorway of the bathroom, confused looks on their faces.

"What's going on with you?" Sullivan asked, his brows furrowed together.

Will stood next to him, crossing his arms and giving me an intense, concerned look.

"I could ask you two the same thing," I retorted, spitting into the sink. I rinsed my mouth with water and turned to face them both straight on.

"What do you mean?" Sullivan asked.

"If you're going to break up with me, at least be man enough to tell me what's really going on."

Will uncrossed his arms and stood up straighter. "Who said anything about breaking up?"

"You guys have been acting weird and distant all night. What the hell am I supposed to think is up?"

They exchanged a nervous look. Sullivan took a step toward me, anxiously rubbing the back of his neck. "Fuck. Will and I were just talking earlier, and I think we're having some issues with jealousy," he said.

Jealousy? The hell …

I stared back at him, my stomach full of knots. "Go on."

Will crossed his arms again, like he was unsure what to do with himself. "Well, sweetheart, the other day, you made Sullivan's favorite pancakes and did his laundry. But then when I asked you to relax with me and watch the game, you blew me off."

"Right, and then just this morning, you kissed Will when you gave him his morning coffee, but you practically rushed right by me when we were all saying our goodbyes," Sullivan added.

It took everything in me not to burst out laughing. My eyes darted between their faces, waiting for them to crack and say they were joking, but they never did. They were dead serious.

"Oh my God, I love you both equally!" I exclaimed, throwing my hands in the air in disbelief. "You two can't be serious."

Sullivan winced, and Will bit the inside of his cheek. "We just thought…"

"Hold on. Let me explain." I first turned to Will. "We happened to have all the ingredients for banana pancakes that day, and I only had a few things I wanted to wash and noticed that Sull hadn't done his laundry yet. That's all. It had nothing to do with me loving him more."

Will nodded, his chiseled, stubbly jaw clenched. It was actually kind of adorable.

"As for you," I said, turning to Sullivan, "I was running late this morning. My first appointment of the day called and asked to move her appointment half an hour earlier, and it totally threw off my whole morning. I wasn't trying to ignore you, I just really had to get out the door."

Sullivan nodded, and the two of them stood there, looking like they practically had their tails between their legs. Walking toward them, I took each of their hands in mine and led them to the bed, where we sat on the edge.

"Listen, I'm sorry," I started, still holding their hands. "I'm not trying to be harsh. You guys just really freaked me out at dinner. I thought you were going to leave me for each other."

Sullivan let out a bark of laughter, and Will placed his other hand on my cheek, running his thumb over my skin. "Never, sweetheart."

Sullivan nodded, placing his hand on my thigh. "It's the three of us. This doesn't work without you."

I nodded, the knots in my stomach finally unraveling at their comforting words. I'm sure to them, my worry about them leaving me was just about as silly as their jealousy was to me. I started to feel the tiniest bit better.

Will guided my mouth to his as Sullivan's hand travelled farther up my thigh. As Will and I began to kiss, Sullivan looked on, caressing my hip and Will's back. Soon, Sullivan brought his lips to one side of my neck, and Will brought his to the other. While their tongues explored my skin, their hands got busy undressing me, slowly and meticulously peeling my silk pajamas over my limbs.

Once I was down to my underwear, Will and Sullivan did the same, and the three of us laid back on the bed, legs and arms intertwined. The feel of their skin against mine was amazing, and I could already feel a damp heat forming between my legs. With each of their stiff lengths pressing into me, my heart started beating faster. I wasn't sure exactly where our night would lead, but I knew that whatever it was, with Will and Sullivan on either side of me, it would be incredible.

I then said the only thing I could think to say, "I'm all yours, boys, do with me what you will."

And they did just that.

Chapter Thirty

Sullivan

"ARE YOU SURE YOU DON'T need anything else?" Will and I tucked Adrienne into bed, and I ran my thumb over her forehead, wanting to make sure she was as comfortable as possible.

"I've got my bowl of ice cream, my rom-com queued up, and two perfect boyfriends who've been totally doting on me for the past two hours. I think I'm good." She smiled and squeezed my hand in hers.

"We're really starting to get this whole period thing down," Will said, giving Adrienne's fuzzy-sock-covered feet one last rub.

Adrienne giggled. "Almost makes me wish that time of the month came more often." As soon as the words left her mouth, she winced and placed a hand on her lower stomach. "Scratch that. Once a month is more than enough."

I placed my hand her shoulder. "Advil's on the bedside table. You're due for your next dose in a couple hours."

"Aye, aye, captain," Adrienne saluted. "More importantly, you two have to give me a play-by-play first thing in the morning. Promise?"

Will and I met eyes, the blood rushing to my cock. Now that the door had been opened for us to explore our sexual connection, Adrienne encouraged Will and me to enjoy tonight. She would sit this night out and give us another opportunity to really figure out how to give each other pleasure. We still wanted her to be a part of it, and she was sad to be missing out, but I'd be lying if I said I wasn't happy to have another night of learning what Will liked without an audience.

"Promise, sweetheart." Will bent down and gave Adrienne a slow, lingering kiss.

My cock stirred again in my pants. Will was just teasing me now. They both were. They knew how crazy it made me to see them touch each other like that.

"Good," Adrienne said when she and Will parted. "Now you two scoot. I've got a movie to watch."

I kissed Adrienne goodbye, and Will and I left her to rest, my heart pounding with anticipation as we climbed the stairs to the other master bedroom.

"God, she's bossy." Will chuckled as I led us inside my room.

"Hush." I gave him a playful shove until he was up against the wall. I put my hand on his scruffy cheek, but he knocked it away. My heart pumped harder remembering the physicality of our first time—the push and pull of us coming together was almost as good as the act itself.

Adrienne was so soft, so giving, so eager to please. Will made me work for it. Every inch I gained with him was hard-won. That did something to me. Plus, it was just really fucking hot.

As much as I loved Adrienne, loved the feel of her soft body against my firm one, loved protecting her, taking care of her needs, I was finding that my love for Will, while newer, was not all that different.

"Been waiting to do this for a while," I murmured, bringing my mouth to his.

His hands pressed firmly against my chest, but rather than shove me away like I was expecting, they sank into my t-shirt, which he used as leverage to pull me closer.

My cock jumped, brushing against his hardening

erection as our lips finally met for a kiss.

"On the bed—strip," I ordered, voice gruff.

Surprisingly Will obeyed, yanking his t-shirt off over his head and unbuttoning his jeans. He sat down on my bed as he worked them down over his hips. His thick cock stood tall and proud and I couldn't wait to get my mouth on it.

When his hand wrapped around it and gave a few strokes, I groaned. "You trying to kill me?"

He smirked. "Were you always this mouthy during sex?"

I grinned at him before pulling my own shirt off over my head. Taking a couple of steps closer, I dropped to my knees on the bed right between his spread thighs and licked the tip of his straining cock.

"You gonna complain about my mouth now?" I asked, looking up at him through hooded, lust-filled eyes.

"Don't stop," he groaned, placing one rough palm against the back of my neck to guide me closer.

"Yeah? You like that" I asked, teasing him with the tip of my tongue against his taut skin.

"Fuck. Take me deeper." Hs hand slid to the back of my head where he moved me up and down, showing me the pace he liked.

He was so commanding, so controlling and confident, and I fucking loved it.

I fisted his cock in one hand and massaged his balls with the other. I knew that some women had a tendency to ignore those, Adrienne generally didn't but other women were so focused on the blow job. Will groaned again, clearly approving of my strategy.

"Better stop unless you want me to blow."

I moved off him with a wet, sucking sound. "We can't have that."

When I rose to my feet, I shoved my own pants and boxers down my hips and Will watched me with expressive eyes as I stroked myself.

"Blowing me got you hot?" he asked. He sounded almost surprised.

"Everything about you gets me hot. Now come here."

He moved closer, scooting toward the end of the bed

where he took me firmly in his hand and treated me to slow, long strokes that almost made my knees buckle. Will watched me with dark, hooded eyes as his hand slid over me.

As much as I didn't want him to stop touching me, I also badly wanted to lay skin to skin in the bed with him.

"Hold that thought," I whispered. My cock was so hard and swollen, I could have hammered the nails into one of our remodel projects.

I grabbed a bottle of lubricant I kept in my bedside table drawer.

"So how the hell does this work?" Will's expression was fucking adorable. He looked legit concerned. He was so lovable, and he had no idea.

"I guess it will be similar to when we prepare Adrienne."

He thought that over. "True. Just don't want to hurt you."

I chuckled. "You just assume you're the top?"

"Fuck yes I do. I'm …"

I touched his hand. "I get it. You're not ready."

He scrubbed one hand over the back of his neck, still watching me.

"And you won't hurt me. I've seen how careful you are with her."

That seemed to please him, and Will grinned halfway before I leaned in and took his lips again. Kissing him so freely like this—it felt forbidden, even though I knew it wasn't, but I was still getting used to it.

Will moved over top of me when I laid back and he took some of the lube and spread it between my cheeks.

"You sure about this?" Will asked, kissing my neck, his stubble scratching my chin.

"Very."

I felt his answering grin against my mouth. "I'll stop if you don't like it."

"I know." I smiled at him.

It felt so natural to be doing this with him—I didn't even question it. But then the time for talking was done, and Will was pressing forward so fucking slowly I thought I would lose my mind.

"Fuck. It's so good," he groaned.

I gripped one hand around his hips and drove him deeper. "Yes. Fuck me. That feels so good, right there."

"Sully," he breathed against my neck.

Will picked up his pace, his hips snapping against mine hitting some place deep inside me that thrummed to life. I moaned, the sound deep and primal. I hardly recognized it.

"Don't stop. Think I'm going to come like this." My cock was trapped between us, but that didn't seem to matter.

"Yeah?" Will sounded breathless, and almost proud.

"Yeah?" I groaned.

He kept up his pace and a few moments later I was climaxing on my stomach in a hot, sticky mess. Will's pace slowed only slightly.

"It's so good, Sull. I'm not going to last."

One more murmured grunt and he followed me over the edge.

After we had cleaned up, we laid side by side in my bed. Will was quiet and I had no idea what he was thinking. Did he like it as much as I did? Did he regret it?

"You okay over there?" I finally asked.

"Never better." Will smiled and all my doubts melted away.

"You're quiet." He was always fairly quiet, but I didn't say that.

"Just processing everything."

That, I understood. This was entirely new territory for us.

"Just don't shut me out, okay?"

He nodded. "I won't."

"Should we go see if Adrienne's still awake?"

"Yeah. Let's go."

Downstairs, we found her curled under the fluffy duvet, her eyes on the TV screen in the otherwise darkened room.

She pressed a button on the remote to mute the TV when she saw us. "Hey. You're back." She smiled.

"Course, baby." I leaned down and kissed her forehead. She hadn't expected us to sleep there, had she?

Will squeezed her bare foot then padded into the

bathroom to brush his teeth.

Adrienne sat up in bed and patted the spot next to her. "Everything go okay?"

I nodded, climbing in beside her. "Yeah."

I wasn't sure how many details she wanted, but Will chose that moment to return and he got into the bed on the other side, sandwiching Adrienne between us.

"Will?" she asked, eyes swinging over to him.

"From my end, it was fucking great."

This seemed to please her curiosity, at least for the time being. "Are you guys going to want to do that all the time now?"

My heart clenched in my chest. What she was really asking was do we still need her. The answer was a huge fucking yes. "Not all the time, no. Maybe once in a great while. I'm fucking sore. His damn dick's too big."

Will and Adrienne both chuckled.

"You're a baby," Adrienne said, smiling at me.

"What she said," Will echoed.

I never imagined we'd be here—after fifteen years of

friendship. And we probably wouldn't be here if it hadn't been for the shove Adrienne gave us. Part of me couldn't believe it. It took a hell of a woman to do what she did. It only showed her love for us, her confidence in what we had. Either way, she'd gone out on a limb and it made me love her that much more.

I fell asleep that night with my arms around Adrienne and a huge smile on my lips.

Chapter Thirty-one

Will

"WAIT, WILL, WHERE are you going?" Adrienne's worried voice stopped me dead in my tracks, just before I could slip out into the garage.

Shit.

I adjusted the strap of my duffel over my shoulder, bracing myself for whatever feelings she was about to lay on me, too.

"And why do you have a bag? Sull, did you know Will was going somewhere?" she called over her shoulder and motioned Sullivan to join us by the door.

"What's going on, Will?" Sullivan furrowed his brows. He was giving me that look he only gives when he's confused—and on the brink of frustrated.

I winced at the looks on both of their faces. This is exactly what I didn't want.

Fuck.

Sighing, I dropped the duffel to the floor and

released a heavy sigh. Adrienne crossed her arms, and the two of them stood there in silence, waiting for me to explain.

Except I didn't really know what to tell them. Everything lately had just gotten so…different. I'd just gotten used to the idea of me and Sullivan taking our own relationship to a new place, and as good as it was, it felt like my world was turning further upside down every day.

I didn't know what the future held, didn't even really know where my friendship with him stood. I wasn't usually the kind of guy who had problems with commitment—when I developed feelings for a woman, I oftentimes fell hard and let her know—but with Sully? I was way out of my depth and that scared the shit out of me.

Things between us were shifting, and they were getting even more confusing with Adrienne in the mix. All I really wanted was a couple days away to clear my head, sort everything out. But I had no idea how to explain any of that to Adrienne and Sull without hurting their feelings. Which is why my first plan was to just sneak out and leave a note. Turns out I'm not as stealthy as I thought I was.

"I'm just going on a fishing trip. I'll only be gone a couple days."

Adrienne nodded slowly and Sullivan crossed his arms. They turned to each other. I did my best to ignore how hurt they looked.

"You weren't going to tell us?" Sullivan stepped toward me. I stepped back. Too close.

I shrugged. "Didn't think it was a big deal."

"Alright, well, enjoy yourself, I guess," Adrienne said, running her hands over her arms. She quickly closed the distance between us and placed a swift peck on my cheek before backing away. Sullivan just nodded. A knot formed in my stomach. I couldn't decide if I wanted him to kiss me goodbye, too.

Before he could decide for me, I slung the duffel over my shoulder and walked out the door, hoping I wasn't making a huge mistake.

The whole drive to the cabin, my mind was going a thousand miles a minute.

From the moment we became best friends, Sullivan and I had always known we wanted to share women. It started out with just hookups with adventurous girls, but we quickly grew out of that and moved on to relationships—mature, loving, adult relationships, the kind of shit we missed out on growing up.

But once Adrienne opened the door to Sullivan and me having sex too, and once we fucking barreled through it, my whole image of how our life would look together was shattered. I'd always felt like the man of the house, and now that I had two people to take care of...

I was still trying to process that.

How could a relationship between three people actually fucking work? What about marriage? Kids? Could I ever give them both what they need? Suddenly every question I'd ever brushed off about ménage was hitting me over the head like a ton of bricks, and I had no fucking clue how to stop it.

***

That evening, I was putting another log on the fire when a knock on the door made me snap to attention.

I walked to the door, mentally preparing to yell at some asshole kids pulling a prank or to let some elderly couple know they were at the wrong cabin. But when I opened the door, my stomach dropped. Standing in front of me were Adrienne and Sully, sopping wet from the rain that had been pouring all day.

"What are you two doing here?" I stood frozen in the doorway, not sure whether to throw my arms around them or step back and give them space.

"Did you really think we were just going to let you run out on us for a couple days without a decent explanation or anything?" Sullivan shook his head, a smile spreading across his face.

"Plus, we're due for a vacay just as much as you are," Adrienne added, her teeth biting into her lower lip.

I smiled and shook my head. "Why am I not surprised? Come inside, you guys are soaked."

They brushed past me and huddled up by the fire. I joined them by the couch, and the moment I sat down, Adrienne took my hand in hers.

"Will, I know you're scared."

I pulled my hand from hers. That wasn't what I was expecting. "No—it's not that, it's just—"

Sullivan placed his hand on my knee and I froze, his

touch simultaneously calming me down and setting me on edge.

"Please, Will, just listen to what we have to say."

I sighed and nodded, my heart pounding so hard I could hear it beating in my ears.

"We get it," Adrienne said, her hand gently taking mine again. "You've always thought that you and Sull only liked sharing women because you were close. What you didn't realize was just how close you two really are. How much you love each other."

I bristled at that word. Love. It was a small one, but it was heavy. Maybe too heavy for me to bare.

"I know it feels like this changes everything," Sullivan said, "but I don't think it has to. Sure, it's unlike any relationship we've ever had before, now that the three of us are truly all together. But I'm starting to think that maybe Adrienne is the girl we've been waiting for all along. The one whose love could show us how much we actually love each other. No other relationship we've been in would this have even come up, that's how we both know how special Adrienne is and how fucking amazing the three of us are together."

He ran his thumb over the curve of my knee, sending shocks of electricity shooting through my body. Adrienne squeezed my hand in hers, and suddenly the two of them were both there, touching me, telling me how perfect we were together—all of it made sense all at once, and it felt like my heart was about to explode out of my chest.

I sighed, looking between them. "First thing we need to go is get you two dry and warm."

They stripped off their wet clothes and we hung them in the bathroom to dry. I stripped down too to join them, and the three of us wrapped up together in blankets closer to the fire.

Adrienne settled in between us, her feet curled up in his lap with her head on my chest. Sullivan and I held hands, resting them on Adrienne's belly, and the three of us nuzzled into each other, enjoying the warmth our bodies made.

Sullivan and I met eyes, and I remembered how I'd left him hanging the night before.

"I love you," I said, holding his gaze. "I don't know how I got so lucky to have you both in my life."

"I love you, too," he said, kissing the top of

Adrienne's head and squeezing my hand in his.

"Love you three." Adrienne smiled.

It was perfect. My two loves, there with me. It was still a bit scary, still a bit unknown, but I was finally ready for whatever future was in store for us.

Just as the thought passed through my mind, Adrienne cleared her throat and sat up, a serious expression on her face.

"I have something to tell you guys," she said, nervously tucking her still damp hair behind her ear.

Sullivan and I exchanged a look, then nodded for her to go on.

"And what I have to say might change everything."

Chapter Thirty-two

Adrienne

MY HEART POUNDING in my chest, I pushed my damp hair away from my forehead before looking up to meet Will and Sullivan's eyes. They were both staring at me, bracing themselves for what I had to say. It was major. Like, bigger than anything that had ever happened in our relationship so far. I just wasn't sure how they were going to take it.

"What's on your mind, sweetheart?" Will ran his thumb under my chin, his eyes soft but attentive, giving me the kind of caring focus so unique to him.

I melted a little under his touch. When he'd tried to sneak out on me and Sullivan earlier, I was sure that he wanted out of this relationship for good. I worried that in pushing him and Sullivan together, I'd pushed him too far, onto another level he wasn't ready for.

That's why I convinced Sullivan that we needed to crash his fishing trip. Sull knew that this cabin was one of his favorites, and it didn't take him long to track down the address. Plus, I wasn't the only one worried about Will.

Sullivan said he seemed off, too, and he agreed it was a good idea to talk him off the ledge.

And as far as I could tell, I think we did. Curled up under a mound of blankets by the fire, it felt like we all finally had let the last of our walls down. When the words "I love you" came out of Will's mouth, I almost burst into tears right then and there. Hearing him be so vulnerable, so vocal about his feelings, was everything I've ever wanted from him. I knew then that I had to tell them my news.

But I couldn't push away the fear that what I had to say would change everything—for good.

"I'm late," I said, looking down at my hands. "I might be pregnant, and I'm never, ever late, only…I don't know whose the baby could be. And I'm not even sure if you guys want kids given the way you grew up."

The room stayed silent aside from the crackling fire and my heartbeat, which was now beating out of control. I cleared my throat, which suddenly felt tight. "I just, I thought you should know."

At first, Will and Sullivan didn't respond, so I kept staring at my hands, waiting for the news to soak in. Just as I was about to add that it was okay if they were upset, that I had reservations about it too, they both abruptly stood up, picking me up in their arms, hooting and hollering with joy. They showered me with kisses, laughing and exclaiming and carrying me around the room.

"Sweetheart, this is incredible! We're going to be a family!"

"You're fucking glowing already, babe."

They continued to celebrate, making jokes about what we were going to name the baby and rummaging around the kitchen to see if there was any leftover champagne—or sparkling cider for me. Eventually, they sat me down on the couch out of fear of harming the baby, quickly deciding that they needed to dote on my every whim.

I sent them into the kitchen to get me a glass of water, taking the moment alone to take a few deep breaths and gather my thoughts.

All of this felt completely bonkers.

I knew I should have been overjoyed to see Will and Sullivan react so positively. This was every girl's dream, right? To find out you're pregnant with the child of the man you love—or in my case, one of the two men, who knows whose baby it is—and to have him be excited and ready to start a family with you? And isn't all this what I wanted? What I'd envisioned from the moment I decided that I wanted to be in this relationship with these two beautiful, amazing, wonderful men?

That might have been true, but it just felt so...soon. We'd just figured out how to be in a relationship of three. How the fuck were we going to figure out how to be four? How would everything work with two dads? What would that life look like for a child? And what right did we have to push our unique arrangement onto another person who didn't ask for it?

After another five minutes of celebrating and coming up short on any champagne or sparkling cider, the guys decided to give up on the fishing trip and just drive home in the rain. Will quickly packed and loaded his stuff up in the car, and the three of us set off, Will and Sullivan still giddy from the news.

My stomach growled, and I poked my head up from the back seat. "Hey, since we didn't find anything at the cabin, do you think we could pick up some fast food on the way? I could really go for a burger and fries right now."

Will and Sull exchanged an amused look.

"Cravings already?" Will asked, a smirk lifting the corner of his mouth.

"That baby's got to be mine, you know I can always go for a burger and fries," Sullivan quipped, swatting Will's arm over the console.

"Yeah, you and the rest of America. Nah, I think I'm the one who knocked her up. Remember last month in the shower? I bet that's when it happened."

"No way, man, the little one is all my doing. I'd put fifty bucks on it."

"Let's make it interesting. Seventy-five."

"Let's make it a hundred!"

I rolled my eyes. "You know that you both own the same business and get paid the same amount, so any money you gamble is just water pouring in and out of the same pond."

They both laughed.

"She's already moody, too! Damn, those hormones work fast."

I chuckled weakly, trying to ignore the growing knot in my stomach. The more Will and Sullivan talked and joked about me being pregnant, the more nervous and uncomfortable I felt. I didn't want to rain on their parade, but I just couldn't bring myself to feel as happy and excited as they did. I sighed and rubbed my temples, leaning my forehead on the cool window.

"Don't worry, babe, we're almost to the drive-thru." Sullivan reached back and squeezed my knee to reassure me. I forced a smile and tried to focus on the one thing I knew I was excited about—a huge ass order of fries.

Once we were done at the drive-thru, the delicious smell of cheap, fried food filling the car, Will hit Sullivan's knee and pointed out the window.

"Hey, look, there's one of those twenty-four-hour drugstores. I bet they'll have pregnancy tests, right?"

Sullivan met my eyes in the rearview mirror. "What do you think, babe? Should we pick one up so you can take it when we get home?"

I nodded, letting my breath out all at once. "Why

not."

"I'm sure they'll have a bathroom there…" Will started, peeking around his seat to look at me.

"If you think I'm about to take a pregnancy test in a drugstore public restroom like some desperate fifteen-year-old, you've got another thing coming," I replied. Will nodded and quickly turned back around. That shut them both up for a bit.

When we got back to our house, multiple pregnancy tests in hand, Will and Sullivan insisted on carrying everything in. They were trying not to be too pushy about it, but I could tell they wanted me to run straight into the bathroom to take the test. Part of me was eager to take it, too, just to get it over with and know one way or the other once and for all. But another part of me was dreading it.

If I *was* pregnant, I knew I'd get even more stressed out about our relationship, and eventually I'd have to talk to them about my fears. But if I *wasn't?* They'd be devastated. And it would break my heart to see them like that.

"Alright, well, here I go," I said, taking the little blue

and white boxes and closing the bathroom door behind me.

"Good luck, babe!"

"She doesn't need luck, she's got my seed in her."

I laughed and shook my head. Even with how nervous I was, my men still managed to make me laugh.

Sighing, I began to open the box and read the instructions. My stomach was churning, and my sweaty fingers made it difficult to open the plastic packaging.

No matter what the results were, things between us were about to change. Forever.

Chapter Thirty-three

Sullivan

"Hang tight, babe. Give me ten minutes, and I'll be back with your lunch."

I kissed Adrienne's forehead, fluffed the three pillows behind her and made my way to the kitchen to get started on her pickle, ham, and marshmallow sandwich. Her weird pregnancy cravings were in overdrive, but I wasn't one to judge. She was having our freaking baby. I was over the moon and ready to do whatever she wanted. Even if that meant making one of the unholiest sandwiches I'd ever heard of.

"How's she doing in there?" Will asked, walking out of the pantry and handing me a bag of marshmallows.

I chuckled and accepted the bag from him with a smile. "A little tired, definitely hungry, but all in all, she's doing great. I think once she's done with lunch, we can move her into the media room. There's a new show she's been itching to watch."

Will nodded, crinkling his nose as I placed a couple

slices of pickle over a bed of marshmallows.

"If I'd known her cravings would be this wild, I might have rethought knocking her up all those months ago."

I arched a brow at him and shook my head. "When are you going to accept the fact that that baby definitely has my genes?"

Before he could answer, I sliced the sandwich in half, set it on a plate and brought it to Adrienne. Sitting on the edge of her bed while she ate, I ran my hand over the firm bump of her belly. It was too early for the baby to be kicking, and I couldn't wait to make contact with our little one.

"He should be around the size of a lime now," Adrienne said between bites, "at least that's what I read online."

"He? You know it's too soon to tell."

Adrienne grinned, taking another bite of her sandwich. "I've just got a feeling."

She had been hesitant at first with the idea of this pregnancy—it wasn't something we'd planned, after all. But once Adrienne saw how happy it made me and Will, she got on board quickly. Now she was practically glowing.

Will joined us in the bedroom with a ginger ale in one hand and a fresh pressed juice in the other. He handed her the ginger ale and set the juice on the bedside table while I fluffed her pillows again.

Adrienne laughed and shook her head. "You two are spoiling me rotten."

"You're carrying precious cargo," I replied.

She smiled, taking another big bite of the disgusting sandwich.

"Once you take a few sips of that ginger ale, we're taking you to the media room."

"We taped a couple episodes of *Kangaroo Moms* for you."

"The new season?" Adrienne's eyes grew wide with excitement. Will and I laughed.

"Suck some of that ale down, and you'll find out."

She narrowed her eyes and slipped the straw between her lips. She took a few small sips before thrusting the glass back at Will. "There. Now let's go see those kangaroos."

She sat up, moving slowly to accommodate her new, growing belly. Will and I exchanged a look, crossing our arms and cocking our heads at her.

"What?" she asked, stopping halfway through the process of hoisting her legs over the side of the bed.

Will and I raised our eyebrows.

"You can't be serious."

"Adrienne, we've talked about this."

She sighed, plopping herself back down on the bed. "Fine."

I turned to Will.

"My turn."

He nodded, and I leaned down for Adrienne to wrap her arms around my neck. With one arm under her legs and the other supporting her back, I straightened, adjusted her so she was comfortable, and carried her to the media room, where I laid her gently down across the couch.

"Happy?" she asked as I draped a blanket over her legs and placed a pillow behind her head.

"Ecstatic."

I brought my mouth to hers, choosing to ignore the strange mixture of vinegar and sugar on her lips.

"You really are glowing, you know that?"

She smiled, placing her hand on her belly.

"I had my reservations at first, but honestly, being pregnant just feels...right."

"It suits you."

Will set her beverages on the coffee table and flipped on the TV. The three of us curled up on the couch together—Will and I making sure to give Adrienne the most room and the best pillows—just enjoying being together as our threesome grew into a foursome.

***

The next morning, the three of us went to Adrienne's doctor for her checkup. At all her previous appointments, only one of us had gone with her because we didn't want to confuse the doctors, but lately it was seeming like having two different men go with her at different times was only raising more eyebrows.

"So, Adrienne, how are you feeling today?" the

doctor asked as he walked through the door, looking down at his clipboard.

"Fine. Normal, I think. A little tired, a little morning sickness, but all in all, not much to complain about."

"Well, that all sounds good. Always good when everything feels…normal." The doctor laid eyes on Will and me as the last word came out of his mouth. He didn't do a great job hiding his confusion.

"I see we've got a full house," he said. "Who do we have here?"

"Dr. Johnson, this is Will, and that's Sullivan." Adrienne's voice didn't carry any hesitation, and that made me grateful. Especially when I thought back on how timid she'd been in the beginning about taking this relationship public.

He reached out and shook our hands, his eyes searching our faces for an explanation. When neither of us gave one, he just barreled through with the rest of the check-up.

"Well, then, Adrienne, why don't you lie back and we'll get this ultrasound going."

Adrienne leaned back, and the doctor squirted the

ultrasound goop on her stomach, moving the wand over her skin to find the heartbeat.

Within moments, that perfect, familiar pulsing sound filled the room. I placed my hand on Adrienne's shoulder, and she quickly clasped hers over mine, grabbing Will's hand with the other. The three of us stood there, listening to the sounds of the new life we'd created together, watching the outline of our baby's little body come in and out of focus on the monitor.

"There's the head," Dr. Johnson said, pointing at a small oval on the screen. "Heartbeat looks and sounds normal. Seems like you have a healthy little baby on your hands."

Adrienne squeezed both of our hands, beaming at us with tears welling up in her eyes.

"He's beautiful."

Dr. Johnson smiled uncomfortably, looking between the three of us.

"We'll know the sex in a few more weeks. So, uh, which one of you two is the father?"

Will and I exchanged a look.

"We're not sure," I said.

"The three of us are going to raise the baby together," Adrienne added.

Dr. Johnson's eyebrows shot up, his head nodding quickly. Clearly we were his first ménage relationship in a while. Scratch that. First ménage relationship ever.

"How progressive of you."

"Pretty common, actually," Will quipped.

At that, Dr. Johnson's mouth fell open, and it took every ounce of self-control in me to not burst out laughing then and there. Will was fucking with him, but the poor guy had no clue what to do or say next.

He quickly wrapped up the appointment, going over when Adrienne needed to come in next and what to expect over the next few weeks. The three of us smiled and nodded politely through his speech, holding it together until we exited the building.

"I was about ready to explain how great the sex is," Will said once we got to the car. "You know that's what he couldn't quite wrap his mind around."

"He's an OBGYN. You'd think he'd be more used to

unusual arrangements like ours." Adrienne shook her head, looking out the window and rubbing her bump.

"A beautiful pregnant woman flanked by a couple studs with no clue whose baby it is? Yeah, I'm sure that's just another Tuesday morning for him." I couldn't resist.

We laughed and kept joking about the appointment for the rest of the ride home.

The life we were building was anything but normal, but it was exactly what I'd always wanted. What I'd been hoping for my whole life, and I certainly wouldn't allow one narrow-minded doctor to ruin our joy.

Chapter Thirty-four

Will

I THOUGHT MY PAST had prepared me for everything. I'd seen a lot of crazy shit in my day. Like my childhood growing up in an orphanage, and even building houses came with its own set of complications and surprises. But nothing, and I mean *nothing*, prepared me for child birth.

I'm not a weak man. But watching Adrienne go through labor? That gave me a whole new level of respect for the bullshit women have to deal with.

Sullivan and I did our fair share of research during Adrienne's pregnancy. We doted on her hand and foot from the moment her pregnancy test came back positive. Bought every book we could find on how to be as supportive as possible in the hospital room, took classes, read endless articles and blog posts online. We knew Adrienne's birth plan like the backs of our hands, and we'd put together the best damn birthing playlist around, complete with classics like "Push It" and "I Will Survive" to play for her in the delivery room.

This pregnancy might have been our first rodeo, but

we made damn sure our girl was safe, comfortable, and supported. After all, we had an advantage most other new moms could only dream of—we had four hands instead of just two.

"You're doing great, sweetheart," I murmured, brushing Adrienne's hair back from her face. "Keep squeezing my hand, you're almost through it."

Adrienne's contractions were coming closer and closer together, and she was handling it like a champ. Even with beads of sweat dotting her upper lip, her blonde hair plastered to her forehead, her face all screwed up in pain and concentration, she was the most beautiful thing I'd ever seen. How she was holding herself together so well was a mystery to me.

"That's it, babe, you're amazing. You're killing it," Sully added his encouragements from the other side of the bed, his voice just as tender and soothing as mine.

Adrienne let out a low, guttural moan as the contraction finally ended. She collapsed back onto her pillow, her chest heaving with exhaustion, and closed her eyes.

"How far apart?" she asked, her words clipped.

"Just under five minutes." I brushed the damp, stray hairs from her face, dabbing her forehead with a cool washcloth.

She sighed and licked her lips. I handed her a cup of ice chips, which she greedily accepted.

"Should I go get the nurse?" Sully's wide eyes flitted to mine. I could tell he was nervous, but he was doing a good job hiding it. For Adrienne. We'd made a pact months ago that we would be her rocks in that room, and so far, we were doing the best that we could.

"Up to you, sweetheart." I turned to Adrienne.

She nodded. "I'm ready."

Her chest was still heaving, the flush in her cheeks extending to her chest. She popped another ice cube into her mouth, and suddenly her face screwed up in pain again, her hand going immediately to her lower back.

"Want me to apply pressure?"

She nodded through her grimace, and I quickly placed my hands on the spot she was just holding. I pressed firmly, watching her face as it softened slightly, happy to do my little part in relieving some of her pain.

Sullivan returned with a nurse, who quickly started asking questions about the contractions, how far apart they were, how much pain Adrienne was in. There had been a shift change since we arrived a couple hours ago, and so Sullivan found himself re-explaining the situation, and that we thought maybe it was time. Throughout the conversation, I caught the nurse giving Sullivan and me a few small, odd looks. Even though Adrienne was practically famous in this hospital for having two baby daddies, this was the first time this nurse had seen us in the flesh.

"Well, Adrienne, it sounds like it's almost time," the nurse said, helping Adrienne get in the proper position on the bed before she examined her. "I'll call Dr. Johnson. He should be here soon. Get ready to meet your baby!"

The nurse hurriedly walked out of the room, leaving the three of us to stare excitedly at each other. *Our baby.* We'd been preparing for this moment for months. And suddenly it was here. It was real. We were about to meet our baby.

Dr. Johnson arrived within a few minutes with a couple nurses in tow. He greeted Sully and me each with a handshake—he'd gotten used to our dynamic after a couple more appointments—and told Adrienne it was almost time and that she should get ready to start pushing soon.

That was our cue.

Sully started the playlist, Salt-N-Pepa encouraging Adrienne to "Push It" right along with us. I stood to Adrienne's right and Sullivan stood to her left, her death grip squeezing both of our hands. Her contractions started again, and Dr. Johnson told her to start pushing. Adrienne stayed quiet and concentrated and focused.

Half an hour of pushing later, the baby was out. A boy. A freaking boy. His cries were music to my ears, and the three of us watched in stunned silence as the nurse cleaned our son up, getting him ready to meet us.

The nurse returned and placed the baby in Adrienne's arms. Tears streamed down her face as she held him to her. Our son. *Our son.* I can't describe the feeling of pride and joy I felt looking at him. I knew it was too early to tell for sure, but I could have sworn he had Adrienne's eyes. The eyes of the woman we loved. I'd recognize them anywhere.

Long after the doctor had gone, the three of us were

still in awe of our new baby. Holding him in my arms for the first time was the most incredible experience of my life. And seeing him with Sullivan? I thought my heart would explode right then and there. The life we'd always wanted for ourselves, for each other, was finally here. We finally had a family of our own. A son. The perfect woman. Suddenly the future was more beautiful than I ever could have imagined.

And the best part?

It was ours.

Epilogue

Adrienne

"OH, COME ON, ref, you've got to be kidding me!" Sullivan threw his hands in the air, the look on his face a familiar and amusing one.

I reached over and placed my hand on his knee as he sank back down into his lawn chair, his brows still furrowed in frustration.

"Sully, you have to relax. They're four. This is hardly competitive soccer."

"But that ref is really tanking this game. Those kids on the other team are mauling our boys. I don't know why Will hasn't said anything to him yet."

"That's because Will is busy coaching. At this age, it's pretty much just herding cats. He's got his hands full."

My gaze strayed over to where my husband stood farther up the sidelines than we were, clipboard in one hand and pencil in the other, his eyes out on the field.

He was a great coach, and that secret soft heart of his made him perfect with the little ones. He'd been working with our son, Ryder, in the backyard since he could walk, and at this point, he was the star of the team. And for a four-year-old, star meant that he was the only one who could kick a ball in the direction he wanted it to go.

One of the little boys on the other team tripped over another kid, and he landed flat on his face, causing the game to take a five-minute break while his mom rushed onto the field to comfort him and calm him down.

I took the break to check on our baby girls, Lily and Penelope, who were sleeping in their twin stroller next to our chairs. When Ryder was two I found out I was pregnant again, a sneaky little surprise. Just when we thought we had a handle on one, two more came our way. But we loved it. Sullivan had decided to stay at home after Ryder, and while he certainly had his hands full once the girls were born, he was a natural. He was an amazing father and loved being a stay-at-home dad while I continued to run my salon and Will kept their real estate business booming.

"Mommy, Mommy, look, I have the ball!" The game had started back up, and Ryder quickly dribbled over and stopped right in front of me on the field, waving in excitement.

"I see that, buddy, good job! Now go, go, go, before the other team catches up to you!"

He nodded, a determined look on his face as he turned to start running up the field, a small mob of four-year-olds trailing behind him. I smiled and shook my head. I could see so much of both of his fathers in him. Sullivan's sweetness and Will's drive. We never did care to do a paternity test, even with as much as my dad pushed us to. It didn't matter to us who Ryder's biological father was, or Lily and Penelope's. What mattered was that the three of us were raising our children together in a loving, caring home. All those traditions Will and Sullivan always wanted? We started them. Family trips? We did them. Big Christmases, we did those, too. We were crushing this whole parenting thing, and every day was an adventure.

When the game ended, Sullivan pulled the cooler out of the car and started to get ready. It was our turn to bring the post-game snacks, and we'd really gone all out. Orange slices and bottles of juice and water, of course, but Sullivan had also made a batch of his famous chocolate and pomegranate energy bites, and he couldn't wait to see how the kids liked them. The girls were awake, so I pulled them both into my lap, balancing one on each knee as we congratulated the sweaty, red-faced boys on their win.

"I'm so proud of you, Ryder! Did you have fun?" I asked.

He nodded, orange juice trickling down his chin as he ate. "I scored a goal, Mommy, did you see me?"

"I did see you, and your sisters did, too. You were a rockstar out there, little man!"

Ryder smiled, the orange peel in his mouth covering his teeth. The girls started laughing, and I quickly snapped a picture. I didn't want to forget any of this. He was already growing up too fast.

"Uh-oh," Sullivan said, spotting Ryder's silly face, "your teeth are gone! Oh no, what are you going to do?" He began chasing him around the field while Ryder shrieked and giggled, yelling back that he didn't want to have teeth anymore. Will noticed them playing and quickly joined the chase, making Ryder shriek even louder. My heart swelled watching the three of them together. My two big men with my one little man. It was almost too amazing to handle.

When Ryder got tired, he came and joined me by the snacks, plopping down on the grass and making faces at his sisters.

Sullivan returned to passing out the snacks while Will chatted with some of the other dads who were already planning strategies for next season. The other moms hesitantly joined us, standing a little off to the side and watching their boys. When we first signed Ryder up for soccer, I was nervous that the other moms wouldn't accept us. Me, especially. The stereotypical soccer mom wasn't necessarily the most open-minded when it came to parenting, and I was nervous that they would look at me with anger or disapproval, thinking that I'd somehow conned two men into having my babies and paying the bills.

But after a few games, I realized that the looks on their faces weren't angry or disapproving at all. No, the way they looked at me, watching Sullivan take care of our girls while Will coached the team, was with envy. They were jealous. What the three of us had might be unconventional, but who wouldn't want another set of hands to help with dishes and dirty laundry? Now, whenever I saw the other moms, I felt sorry for them. They had no idea what they were missing. Never mind having four hands to help around the house instead of two. My men were the perfect complements to each other, each one filling in where the other fell short.

It might be true that the perfect man doesn't exist. But between my two men, I think I've found perfection.

Smiling, I glanced at my phone to check the time. "We better get packed up. Time to go meet Grandma and Grandpa for lunch."

Sullivan nodded, grinning conspiratorially, and lifted Penelope out of my arms, planting a kiss on her chubby cheek, before placing her into her car seat, and then doing the same with Lily.

My parents had moved closer right after Ryder was born—in a custom home built by Will and Sullivan. We'd developed a tradition of having lunch together after soccer. In fact, they rarely missed a game. Sometimes we went out for pizza, and other times for subs.

But because it was Will's birthday next week, and Mom and Dad learned that he'd never had a surprise party growing up, they got this crazy idea in their heads that they wanted to throw him a little surprise party today after soccer.

I knew that right now Mom was probably putting

the finishing touches on the cupcakes or tying up bunches of balloons, and Dad was likely firing up the grill. It made me so happy how accepting my parents had become of my two sweet husbands. It had taken a few years, but now my mom and dad both regarded Will and Sullivan as the best sons-in-law you could ever ask for. And they were in love with their new role as grandparents, too.

As I stood, Will helped me to fold up my chair. "You looked good out there, coach." I gave his butt a playful slap.

"Hey now ..." He grinned. "There are children present."

I raised one eyebrow. "Guess you'll have to teach me a lesson later."

Still smiling, Will leaned down to give me a quick kiss. "You promise?"

Sullivan walked up at just that exact moment and said to Will, "Yeah, we both promise."

My God, what these men do to me.

About the Author

Lola Leighton is the pseudonym for a *New York Times* bestselling romance author who wanted to write steamier stories that her mother is most definitely not allowed to read.

23682855R00205

Made in the USA
Columbia, SC
11 August 2018